GHOULISH BOOKS
San Antonio Texas
www.GhoulishTales.com

Ghoulish Tales—Issue #1
Copyright © Ghoulish Books 2023
(Individual stories are copyright by their
respective authors)
All Rights Reserved

ISBN: 978-1-943720-91-0

ARTWORK CREDITS

Cover and Interior Artwork
by Betty Rocksteady

CONNECT WITH US

Patreon:
www.patreon.com/pmmpublishing

Website:
www.GhoulishTales.com

Facebook:
www.facebook.com/GhoulishMagazine

Twitter:
@GhoulishTales

Instagram:
@GhoulishBookstore

Newsletter:
www.PMMPNews.com

Linktree:
www.linktr.ee/ghoulishbooks

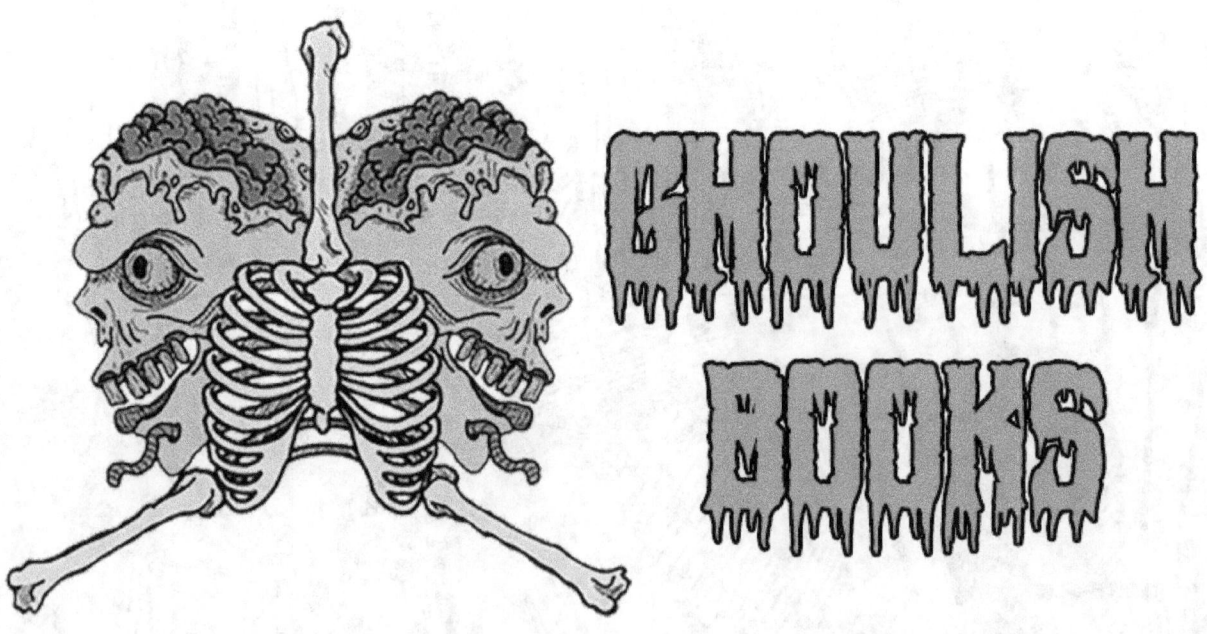

A THANK YOU TO OUR 2023 KICKSTARTER SUPPORTERS

A. C. Knight, A. J. Conway, Ada Ostrokol, Adrian, Adrian Shotbolt, Agatha A., AingealWroth, aj, Alejandro Figueroa, Alex Ebenstein, Alex Rodriguez-Acevedo, Alexander (Beast) Luthy, Alvaro Rodriguez, Amanda Hard, Amy Gijsbers van Wijk, Amylou Ahava, Andi, Andrew Hilbert, Andrew Kozma, Andrew Shaffer, Andy Martino, Angel Leal, Angel Luis Colon, Anna Dodson, Anna M Valles, Anthony Bowman from The Frankencast, Ariana Limone-Ryan, Audry Olmsted, Austin Hofeman, Austin Wilson, Autumn Pike, Ava Dickerson, Bea Goode, Becca Futrell, Becky Robison, beedeebrave@gmail.com, Benoît Lelièvre, Betsy Nicchetta, Betty Rocksteady, Beverly Bambury, Bill, Bill Kohn, Bill Sizemore, Bill T, Bob DeRosa, Bob Pastorella, Bobby H., Brad Sanders, Brandon & Candice Held, Brandon Santana, Brent Jones, Brian Huff, Brian King, Brian M, Brooke Gessner, Brooke Kennelley, Buffalo Billie, C Billow, C. D. Kester, C.R. Langille, Cai Murphy Ritenour, Campbell R., Caroline, Caroline Coriell, Carter, Cemetery Gates, Charles M., Charlie Wellman, Charlotte Platt, Chess Ruby, Chris Baumgartner, Chris Williams, Christian D Leaf, Christina Morris, Claire, Clay and Meade Byers, Clay McLeod Chapman, Collin Martino, Corey Doerr, Craig Hackl, Cynthia Petersen, Dai Baddley, Dakota Reinhart, Damia Torhagen, Dan and Summer Smith, Dan Scamell, Daniel Moore Hinton, Daniel Vlasaty, Daniel, Trista, and Eleanor Robichaud, Danielle Stachnik, Darcie Nadel, Dave Urban, David Cross, David Demchuk, David Hoffman, David K., David Myers, David Raposa, David Worn, Dawn Colclasure, Daxh A., Dead Fishie, Dennis Tafoya, Denver Grenell, Destiny Andrews, Diversity in Horror, Don Lee, dwbrid80@gmail.com, Dylan B, E. M. Roy, Ed Grady, Elizabeth Guilt, Elizabeth R McClellan (popelizbet), Em, Emily Walter, Emma J. Gibbon, Emmy Teague, Eric K, Eric Raglin, Erica H. Walsh, Erica Robyn, Erik Smith, Ethan Hutchinson, Eve Harms, Francesca Ripley, Franco Guarino, Frederick Rossero, Full Throttle Sound, Gage Gaiss, gallenmartin@gmail.com, Gardner Linn, Gareth Jones, Gary N. Parenteau, Gavin P, Geoff Emberlyn, Giusy Rippa, Grant Longstaff, Hadley S., Hailey Claire Hull, Hailey Piper, Haley H., Hana Correa, Hannah Janda, Holly Benavente, House of Blood, How is that Night?, Ian Chant, Ifeanyi Esimai, Illeana, izsch2, J Manchester, J.M. Brandt, Jacen Leonard, Jakii Culver, James Fitzsimmons, James Wilson, Jamie J., Jarne Van Vooren, Jason McCoy, Jay Slayton-Joslin, Jeanine Long, Jeff Meyers, Jeffrey C., Jenny Underwood, Jeremiah Israel, Jerry Purdon, Jes Malitoris, Jesse Zurlino, Jessica McHugh, jhenrymckeen@yahoo.com, Joanne A., Jodee Stanley, Joe butler, John Alex Hebert, John Baltisberger, Jonathan Brown, Jonathan Gensler, Jonathan Knell, Jonathan L, Jonathon M. Smereka, Joseph Z., Josh & Karin Swope, Josh Buyarski, Joshua Cooper, Justin Lewis, Justin Lutz, K Petrin, Kalyn W, Katlina Sommerberg, Kayli Scholz, Kelly Hoolihan, Kenny Endlich, Kevin H., Kevin Lemke, Kevin Thomas, Kevin Wadlow, Kirsten Murchison, Kris Breighner, Kristina Meschi, Kye, Kyle J Shepherd, L.P. Hernandez, Laura Goostree, Laurel Hightower, Lauren Bolger, Lauren Carter, Lauren Roberts, LC von Hessen, Leftie Aubé, Leslie Twitchell, Linda and Larry Winzenread, Lionel Ray Green, Lisa Westenbarger, Logan Moore, Lottie Biscotti, LT Williams, Lunar Violet, LuPa, M Baker, M. Allen, M.Bouckaert, Madeleine Koestner, Mae Murray, Maggie L. Omaña, Magnus Lima, Malachi Abell, Mandy Bublitz, Margaret A., Mari B, Maryanne Chappell, Mason Hawthorne, Matt Brandenburg!!, Matt Henshaw, Matt Ramsey, Matt Stepan, Matthew Walker, Max B. , Megan Kiekel Anderson, Megan Mccullum, Mel Layos, Melissa Cox, Mia Tylia, Michael A. Cook, Michael Cieslak, Michael G. O'Connell, Michael Louis Dixon, Michael Paul Gonzalez, Michael R., Michelle Glatt, Michelle Quaynor, Miguel Myers ATx, Mike McCrary, MindyLeeReads, morda sam, MortalTraveler, Najwa Red, Nate Bondurant, Nic Knack, Nick Kolakowski, Nicolas, Nicole Sadenwater, Niko Thompson, Nikolas P. Robinson, Nisha Hollis, Norbert Böhm, Paige Holland, Pat Bevins, Pat S., Paul Buchholz, Paul Cardullo, Perry M, Polyeurythane, Preston F., Prince Eric Vickers, R. C. Hausen, Rain Corbyn, Ray Reigadas, ReArcangeli, Regino, Rena Mason, Reneé Hunter Vasquez, Renee Pickup, Res Bratton, Ria Hill, Riley R., River Hudgins, River Onei, RJ Joseph, Robbie Dorman, Robert Mikkelson, Roger Venable, Rose O., Ryan Booth, Ryan C., Ryan C. Bradley, S. Kay Nash, S. White, Sadie Cocteau, Sam Kurd, Sam Logan, Samantha Eaton, Sandra Ruttan & Brian Lindenmuth, Sara Corris, Sarah McGinley, Sarah P, Schatzi, Scott Adlerberg, Scott Hastings, Sean Ford, Sean Leonard, Sebastian Ernst, Sergey Kochergan, Seth, Shane Hawk, Shannon Bradner, Sharon Levy, Shelly Lyons, Sheri White, Shrader Thomas, Siobhan Dunlop, Siobhan Thomas, Sirrah Medeiros, Skip Zepeda, Sofia Ajram, Sophia Lebar, Sophie Newman, Stephanie Brantner, Steve Irwin, Steve Loiaconi, Steve Pattee, Steven Campbell, stevenroy@gmail.com, Stevie McJigglemeats, Suppi, Susan Jessen, Tai Black, Taliesin Neith, Tanya Semmons, Tav Jackson, Tenebrous Press, Teresa B. Ardrey, The ARC Party, The Blerd Newsletter, Theresa Derwin, Thomas Joyce, Thurston Howell VIII, Tim Meyer, Tobias Carroll, Todd Keisling, Tom Deady, Tore Nielsen, Trevor Olsen, Victor Adam Garcia, Victoria Nations, Warren Wagner, Webberly Rattenkraft, William Jones, Witchyjazzy, Yve Budden, Zach Low, and Zachary Locklin,

A SPECIAL THANK YOU TO OUR PATREON SUPPORTERS

Adam Rains, Adrian Shotbolt, Alice Phelan, Allison Henry-Plotts, Amanda Niehaus-Hard, Antony Klancar, Betty Rocksteady, Bob, Bob Pottle, Brad Sanders, Brett Reistroffer, Brian James Freeman, Bridget Brave, Chazzaroo, Chris Baumgartner, Claudia J Parker, Clay Waters, Cullen Wade, Dan Howarth, Daniel Scamell, Dave, David Demchuk, David Perlmutter, DeerNoises , Drew Purcell, Emma Williamson, Erin Murphy-Jay, Eve Harms, Fox Morphis, gengar, George Daniel Lea, Grant Longstaff, Gregory A. Martin, Ian Muller, Jack Smiles, James (Tony) Evans, Jampersand, Jason Kawa, Jennifer McCarthy, Jesse Rohrer, Jessica Leonard, Jessica McHugh, Joe Z, Joey Powell, John Foster, Jose Triana, Julie Cyburt, Kev Harrison, Kevin Lovecraft, Leslie Hernandez, Lisa, Matt Neil Hill, Matthew Booth, Matthew Brandenburg, Matthew Henshaw, Michael Kazepis, Michael Louis Dixon, Miguel_myers_atx, Mistina Picciano, Myrmidon, Nathan Weaver, Nichole Neely, Night Worms, Nikolas P. Robinson, Patrick Tumblety, Rachel Cassidy, Rebecca, Richard Staving, Rob Gibbs, Robin Lanehurst, Roger Venable, S. Kay Nash, Sammynona , Samuel Peirce, Scott Adlerberg, Scotty Nerdrage, Shannan Ross, Shelby MacLeod, Sheri White, Sherry Solorio, Steve Ringman, Steven Campbell, Stewie, This Is Horror, Thomas Joyce, Todd Keisling, Traci Kenworth, Webberly Rattenkraft, Will Griskevich, Will Wellman, William Hull, and Zachary Ashford,

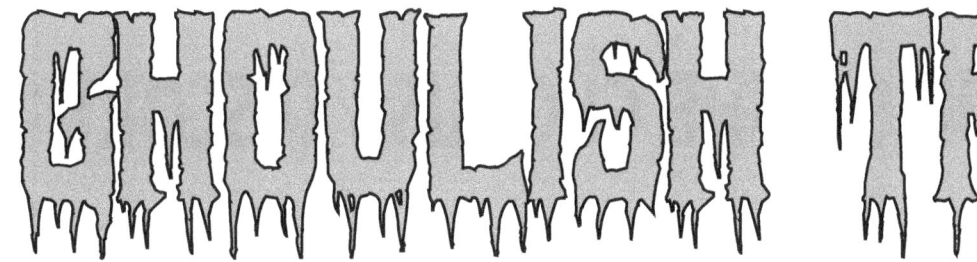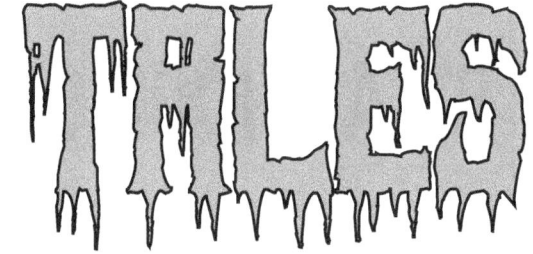

Issue #1

TABLE OF CONTENTS

WHO WANTS TO READ SOME SPOOKY GODDAMN STORIES?

EVERY TIME I'M interviewed, I get the same question. *Why horror?* This is especially true for outlets who aren't already dedicated to horror coverage. Local newspapers, generic pop culture websites, etc. They're always fascinated why I've chosen to dedicate my life to horror. It's hard for them to wrap their head around the idea. The question comes up a lot at popup events or at our horror-themed bookstore, too. Especially when it's nowhere near October. When it's October, they definitely get it. They think we're taking advantage of Halloween. But when they find out our annual horror fest—the Ghoulish Book Festival—is held in the *spring,* that only further baffles them. Why would anyone like horror outside of "the spooky month"?

The truth is, I can't remember a time in my life that wasn't surrounded by the horror genre. I grew up with much older siblings who had slashers playing on television nonstop. Plus I had an aunt—my mom's best friend—who was just as obsessed, and as I got slightly older she would burn pirated underground horror movies onto blank discs and let me borrow them whenever we visited. My earliest movie memory is the OG Evil Dead trilogy. I watched them nonstop, mesmerized. At this point, it's safe to say they've found a way into my DNA, and they are here to stay.

There was no moment where I decided, "I now love horror." I emerged from the womb with a Freddy Kreuger glove. Loving horror comes just as naturally to me as breathing oxygen.

All of this is to say that it was a no-brainer that we would eventually launch *Ghoulish Tales,* a magazine dedicated to celebrating everything spooky. Everything I love and cherish.

I am writing this introduction near the end of June 2023. When we initially announced this new magazine, our intention had been to publish the inaugural issue back in April to coincide with our second-ever Ghoulish Book Festival in San Antonio. As you can probably surmise, things did not happen according to plan. Rather than publish the first issue of the magazine on time, this is what we did instead: hosted a book festival, opened the only horror-themed bookstore in the San Antonio area, and got married. April was an insane month, to put it lightly, and it has taken both myself and Lori Michelle (Booth!) several months to recover from the consequential burnout.

But here we are. No more excuses, right? You aren't here for that.

Ghoulish Tales Issue #1 is finally in your disgusting little hands, and I couldn't be more excited. It is no longer the Spring Issue but the Summer Issue now. In this magazine you will encounter 8 short stories and 2 essays. Going through the slush was an incredibly exhausting process. For issue 1, we received 1,195 submissions to consider, which we somehow narrowed down to the 10 you are about to read. Many of the authors we accepted were names I was not familiar with at the time, but now I consider myself a fan for life. It is my hope that, after you finish this issue, you will feel the same way.

I will not waste any more page space here. You came for some spooky goddamn stories, and some spooky goddamn stories are what you're going to get.

Enjoy the ride, ghouls.

—Max Booth III

Subscribe to
THE GHOULISH TIMES

Keep yourself updated with everything going on in the world of GHOULISH by subscribing to our newsletter, The Ghoulish Times!

Essays, interviews, and even occasional fiction! Plus, photos of our cute dogs.

Everybody in your neighborhood is already subscribed.

WHY AREN'T YOU?

https://theghoulishtimes.substack.com

WHO BRINGS A BABY?

Clay McLeod Chapman

WHAT KIND OF parent brings their baby to a horror movie? A nine o'clock screening on a Monday night, no less . . . If you can't afford a sitter, then I'm sorry, you shouldn't shell out fifteen bucks for a flick. Put that money aside for this kid's therapy bills, which will no doubt be coming, thanks to mom and dad dragging their child's diapered ass to some slasher rehash and ruining the movie for the rest of us.

Remember when theaters used to be a sacred space? Holy temples for celluloid? The point is to immerse yourself in the filmgoing experience. The world outside the cineplex simply melts away as soon as the lights go down. You are now lost in that tenebrous cosmos, your very soul elevating itself out of your body, drifting along with everyone else from the audience and entering that vast expanse of the silver screen, as if the pearly gates just opened up to us all.

We go for that cinematic rapture.

But now we have cell phones to contend with. Texting and blooping and bleeping all through the movie. Once I was forced to listen to some preteen drama queen prattle on with her gal pal from the seat behind me, gossiping over the phone rather than watch the movie we all paid to see—that *I* paid to see. *Why piss over the film for the rest of us?* I shouted over my shoulder so that everyone in the theater could hear. *Why not just stay at home, young lady? Netflix and chill out somewhere else? Do something—anything—other than step into my* temple and blather on about whose boyfriend is cuter than whose during my cinematic sermon.

Guess who received their own round of applause from the audience after sending that girl out of the auditorium in tears?

Someone needs to protect this hallowed space from unruly customers. *Someone* needs to hold the line. The very integrity of the filmgoing experience is at stake and if you won't risk your life to defend it, then what in God's name is the point of going to the movies anymore?

But nothing—I mean nothing—desecrates a film quite like listening to the four alarm fire of some wailing baby overtake an entire auditorium. Sound carries differently in a theater. It doesn't matter where you sit: if your kid is bawling in the back row, we're all going to hear it.

Case in point: Tonight, less than ten minutes into the film, I sense this sniveling infant from somewhere deep in the darkness. I can't pinpoint the exact location. The whimpering is coming from somewhere in the rear of the theater. It begins with a chainsaw sputter, just a few tugs from this kid's lungs, like yanking back on the pull-chord of a power tool. But once that wet engine gets revving, I know in my bones this little bastard is going to roar all through the movie.

Where is it? I peer over my shoulder to try pinpointing this family. All I see are the silhouettes of heads. The theater is practically empty, save for a few scattered shadows. No bouncing baby bopping along in the darkness, even if I can hear it. Am I the only one bothered by its staccato sobbing? It's only growing in volume now, gaining momentum with every clenched breath. At a certain point, just as a courtesy, you'd think mom or dad might heft their newborn foghorn into the lobby. Just don't, you know, *stay*. Don't sit in your seat and act like nothing's happening, *nothing wrong here at all*, as your kid shrieks and shrieks and shrieks.

Who's following the storyline anymore? I certainly can't. Is anyone paying attention to the movie? I could alert the manager and complain, but that pimple-faced excuse for a spine won't do more than stutter through some scripted excuse for a scolding. They never do a thing.

No, I'll take matters into my own hands. I'll answer that baby with my own battle-cry:

Sssh! I hiss over my shoulder. That should do it. Loud and clear. I'm completely anonymous here. Mom and dad will never know it was me, sitting in the third row, second from the aisle, but they'll know that we the people of this movie theater have collectively spoken.

But this baby . . .

It won't stop bawling. Jesus, how big are this kid's lungs? The sound of its crying expands and contracts, eclipsing everything onscreen. We've now entered a new phase of wailing—short, glottal retorts that pepper the theater in these auditory depth charges. If this were a war movie, I'd imagine the crying was just another sound effect. But no—these sonic hand grenades are coming from behind me, blasting at my ears. Total surround sound.

So I do what any rational-minded moviegoer would do. I simply turn to the back of the theater and shout: *Some of us are trying to watch the movie!* That'll shut it up. Take that, tyke!

But this baby . . .

Now the crying is closer. Where the hell are they? It's as if the fam has moved forward a few rows, just to mess with me. Toy with me. The blackened space compresses itself so it now sounds like that caterwauling kid is sitting in the row right behind me, bawling just at my back.

Over my shoulder.

At my neck.

Something nicks my left ear. Just the slightest slice over the lobe. It stings, my shoulder springing up in a defensive reflex. There's a warm trickle dribbling down the length of my neck.

I'm bleeding. How am I bleeding?

This baby . . .

Now the crying creeps into my right ear.

There's a thin wriggle against the lobe and I can't help but imagine a worm working its way through the canal. I turn in time to catch a passing glance at a pale, pudgy pinkie finger reeling back into the blackness behind me.

Now the crying comes from up front. In the aisle. The baby just won't stay still. I can't nail down the sound anymore. It's everywhere and nowhere all at once, circling around me.

Closing in.

Something brushes against my right ankle, slicing through my sock. Both my legs pitch upwards as I scream, sending popcorn into the air.

Sssh! Other audience members hiss back, as if I'm the problem. But there's something strange about the timber to it. It doesn't sound like a pissed off patron. They're mocking me.

Somebody help, I shout. But no one answers. Searching the theater, I notice none of the silhouettes I'd spotted before are there anymore. Where did everyone go? Everyone else in the audience has disappeared . . . if they were even there at all. A very cold thought enters my mind: What if those shadows weren't actually people? What if I've got the whole theater to myself?

I plunge into the row of folding seats. Old soda seeps through my pants. Or maybe it's blood. I've got a good view of the floor now, covered in candy wrappers and shriveled popcorn.

I'm going to wait for that baby. This time, I'll see it coming. This time, I'll be ready.

Where is it where is it where is it where . . . I hear the soft pads of its paws peeling off the sticky floor, all covered in coagulated cola, but I can't see it. *Where is it where is it where* . . .

The vaguest shape slips past me. An albino flash. Was that a rat? Are there mice in the movie theater? It's not too late to escape. I can just crawl into the aisle and run for the exit.

Where is it where . . .

There! A pair of eyes glint in the dark, as gleaming as the silver screen. It's a baby alright, crawling on its hands and knees, but not like any newborn I've ever laid eyes on before. I don't think this child has ever seen the sun in its entire life. Its skin is practically translucent, mottled in multicolored tumors. The cysts shimmer in the dim glow cast from the movie projector.

Wait—those aren't tumors. Those are Jujubes.

That gelatinous candy that always gets caught in your molars. Teens toss them at the screen to see if they'll stick, but this pustulating infant is covered in them. A rainbow-hued leper. There's a speckling of stale popcorn flecking its limbs, nodules of kernels clustered across its shoulders, like lopsided vertebrae all over its back.

The baby's blistered lips—*Do I still think this is a baby?*—are dusted in white nonpareils—those are Sno-Caps—and I can't help but think it's erupting in abscesses.

Something slashes the backside of my hand. I cry out in pain and the crowd hisses, *Sssh!* But it's not coming from the audience. There is no audience. This is an imitation of a shush, a cruel mimicry of my own hiss getting echoed back at me . . . and it's coming from all around. *Sssh!*

There's another baby in the aisle now.

And another.

Their eyes are silver, as blinding as the screen itself. I count three of them—no, make that four—five—each scabbed in candy from the concession stand, Swedish Fish and Mike & Ikes and Junior Mints and Raisinettes and Goobers and Skittles and Gobstoppers and M&Ms . . .

There was never just one.

They're closing in on me now, slowly crawling across the floor on their hands and knees, each inch forward punctuated with the tacky peeling of their skin.

They're not crying anymore.

Oh God, they're giggling.

Sssh . . . Sssh . . . Sssh . . .

This theater was never my temple . . . It's their hunting ground.

RUNE THE ~~OWL~~ DEMON

LIFE IN THE DEMON'S GIZZARD

Betty Rocksteady

THE RAIN POUNDS against the window, fills the silence between the sisters. Tess is on the floor, swirls of dark hair falling into her face, sorting through teetering stacks of VHS tapes. "What should we watch first?

"I still don't know why you kept *all* of those. You've way too attached to this junk." Nicole slouches on the sofa behind a TV tray covered in snacks—cheese, crackers, chips, meat. A feast for her last night here with Tess.

"I can't just get rid of them. It's our childhood."

"Honestly, I'd like to get rid of a lot of our childhood."

Tess shuffles the tapes. Mostly kid stuff. A lot of it taped off the TV, Tess and Nicole's childish scrawls labeling the contents. But there's also at least a dozen brightly-colored cartoon tapes, off-model drawings of Betty Boop, Mickey Mouse, Felix the Cat, all the classics. "Really? I'd love to go back. Just for a little while. No responsibilities. And Mom and Dad, of course, to have them back."

"You barely have any responsibilities now. That's been your life for the last 27 years."

"Hey, remember Rune?" Tess holds up a tape. The cover isn't colorful like the other ones; a black scrawl of ink against a white background. An owl leers out, all big black eyes and ruffled feathers. "You used to love this one. Maybe we should watch this first, and then a movie?"

"*Did* I love it? Honestly, I don't remember this shit the way you do." Nicole watches Tess' face, then sighs, softens very slightly. "OK. Pick one. I can't stay up watching cartoons all night. I have to get up super early for my flight tomorrow."

"You don't have to. You could stay."

The rain fills the silence again. Tess' lower lip starts to shake, and her eyes brim with tears that don't quite spill over. Nicole says nothing, looks back at her phone.

"Nicole," Tess starts.

"Pick something to watch, Tess. I'll watch one cartoon."

"I can't decide. You pick."

"Put on the owl one. I really don't care. I don't remember any of them. It's all new to me."

Tess smiles, showing too many teeth. "OK, awesome. You really did like that one when we were kids. I remember watching it all the time."

"Are you sure the VCR even works?"

"Yeah, I use it every now and then, it works fine." She shoves the tape into the machine and it whirs as it rewinds. "It's only 22 minutes, just three cartoons. We can probably watch something else after. You don't have to get up that early."

The cartoon clunks as it finishes rewinding. Tess presses play, then climbs up on the couch next to Nicole and the untouched snack board. Nicole types something into her phone, smiles faintly. Tess shoves crackers and cheese into her mouth. "It's good," she says. Nicole nods.

The cartoon starts with a cheery scream of trumpets. Swaying grey trees surround a title screen, white letters on a black background: *Albert Lyster presents Rune the Demon.*

"He's a demon?" Nicole asks. "I thought he was an owl."

"I guess he's both. I know we watched these but I don't remember much else. Remember when we were kids? We'd sit on the floor in front of the TV."

"Yeah, while Mom screamed at Dad in the kitchen."

Tess doesn't reply to that. The cartoon starts. Well, it's not a cartoon yet. It's a regular film. Black and white, shades of grey bleeding into each other. A hum of staticky silence as a man scribbles away on a drawing board. A glimpse of his writing. Not quite letters, maybe symbols or maybe just practice loops of his pen. After a moment, he flips to a blank page and turns to greet the audience. His hair is neatly combed back, dark eyes sunken in his face. The white expanse of paper behind him is ripe with potential. He smiles.

"I thought this was a cartoon?" Nicole picks up a cracker but doesn't eat it.

"Shh."

The cartoonist introduces himself as Uncle Al and dips his fountain pen into the inkwell. "Cartoons are a remarkable art. A curve here and a swish there, and you have a funny little character." His pen dances across the page, lines and circles, a smear of black ink, and Rune appears.

"He doesn't look like an owl *or* a demon really." Nicole frowns.

"Yeah, these cartoons are so old, the language isn't really there yet. Like, Rune is one of the first cartoons *ever*. It's kind of cool, right? Just raw creative energy."

Rune dances across the page, his wings changing shape and size, his proportions stretching and distorting. "Creation is the most important part of life, one of the most fundamental human urges. Creating, and sharing your creation with others. The audience is just as important as the artist. Because without one, how would the other exist?" Uncle Al grins. "You can do anything in a cartoon. Makes you feel like you can shape real life just the same. Wouldn't that be fun?" Rune nods his agreement, eyes swirling with darkness.

"I don't know how you can watch this shit," Nicole says. "It's starting to give me a headache."

"And when I say anything, I mean *anything*." A few swirls of his pen and a hammer appears. The handle has a real weight to it, heavy and wooden, the claw sharp and dangerous-looking. Nicole's

back stiffens. A few loops of the pen and a goofy wide-eyed farmer appears and picks up the hammer. He chases Rune across the blank page for a few seconds, and the hammer grows in size as he lifts it over his head and throws it at Rune. Feathers fly, blood squirts, Rune is flattened.

"Ugh," Nicole says.

A pause on the squished mass, a hesitation, a vibration, and then Rune pops back up into shape, eyes swirling, beak sharp. Uncle Al blots out the farmer with a sea of black ink. "See! Anything can happen in a cartoon! And if you don't like it, you can change it. Just like in real life. All right, Rune, take a bow and get back in there." Rune bows and hops back in the inkwell. Jazzy trumpet music swells up again as the credits roll.

"Ugh, that was awful. I don't even get it. There's no plot. I didn't even like these when I was a kid."

"Yes you did! We watched this all the time." Tess shoves more crackers in her mouth and Nicole looks closely at her before speaking.

"My memories of being a kid aren't as happy as yours are, Tess. I don't think yours are even really as happy as you think they are."

Tess turns her attention back to the screen. "That one was weird, but I think the other ones must have been better or we wouldn't have watched it all the time."

Nicole sighs. "I don't think I can watch any more of this, Tess. I'm going to head to bed."

"No, come on. It's only 22 minutes. You promised." Tess slides closer on the couch, drapes herself across Nicole's lap. "Please. You make me feel like you hate me. I don't want you to go to bed. I want to hang out with you. I don't want you to go at all. You don't have to go."

Nicole puts a reluctant hand on Tess' back. "I can't stay forever. I have a life to get back to."

"Yeah, well, I have nothing. I've lost *everything*. Mom and Dad are dead, you're leaving, I'm all fucked up and I can't do this alone." Tess buries her face in Nicole's lap as the jazzy intro music to the next cartoon begins.

Nicole tries to extract herself from Tess' grip and goes limp instead when she can't. "I've been here three weeks. I've done everything I can to help you get this place cleaned up and get some resources in place for you. You've fought me every step of the way. I don't know what you want from me but I can't give you any more. I can't live your life for you."

The next cartoon starts, neither girl watching it. Rune walks through a dark forest as tiny creatures skitter by. His feathers shift as his body sways from side to side.

"They were your parents too."

"Yeah, they were, and I spent years unfucking myself up from them and building a life that I actually enjoy."

On screen, Rune scuttles up a tree until only his eyes peer out from the leaves. A grinning mouse family dances across the forest floor. Trumpets blare as Rune plunges down from the tree and swallows them whole. Faint squeals beneath the music. Rune burps, and one of the mice leaps from his throat and scurries away.

"Let me breathe."

Tess sits up reluctantly. "I don't know why you're being like this. They *were* good parents. They did everything for me, they would have done everything for you too."

"Yeah, they did do everything for you, but I don't think that did you any good. They were both fucking nuts. I loved them, of course I did, but Mom's mental illness made her a fucking nightmare to live with and I'm lucky I escaped. I'm sorry you didn't, but now is your chance to build a better life for yourself. Do the therapy, take it seriously, take advantage of the money you inherited—this is a good thing. You don't have to end up like her."

A wolf follows Rune through the forest, laughing as he creeps through the bushes. Its' eyes are hungry, but Rune's are hungrier. The wolf is huge, a mess of scars and matted fur. Rune is clever. Every time the wolf gains an upper hand, Rune shifts and his body blurs and something changes. Tess' eyes are shiny, cracker crumbs on her chin. "It's so weird the way these old cartoons were. Like you just said, the way they don't really have a plot. Like Rune got so popular for a while, and everything went totally cookie-cutter. Not as big as Mickey Mouse, but way different from this stuff. God, it must be so weird for the cartoonist, do you think?"

"What are you talking about?"

"You know, how like you make something, you have an idea for it and back then cartoons were like brand-new, so he was doing this crazy, experimental thing and then it gets all popular and completely out of his hands. Like it has nothing to do with his original idea, it expanded so far past that. These ones have that initial creative spark, though. The *real* stuff, you know? Like where does that spark even come from, do you think? Did he *invent* Rune, or did he just pluck him out of the ether somehow? The collective unconscious, I don't know. Do you know what I mean?"

"I don't give a fuck about the cartoon, Tess. Is this really want you want to be talking about?"

Rune's legs grow beneath him, strange sharp angles, too many joints, his squat body teetering on top of them as he runs through the dark wood. A mob of animals follow him, lit candles clutched in their hands, murmuring under their breath.

"It's just weird, right, the way something can spin entirely out of the creator's control?" Tess' forehead is shiny with sweat. Her words are coming faster and faster. "I don't know. Maybe it sounds really weird but I feel, like, *connected* to that cartoonist. Do you think it's because I watched it so much as a kid? I feel like I know what he's thinking. I feel like he wanted Rune to be something, and things got out of his hands and he was so angry about it. It got popular, but I bet he never even got paid for those later cartoons. I bet that isn't even what he wanted, that thing he said, how the audience is important too. He thought he wanted Rune to be successful, but what he really wanted was for Rune to be *seen*. You know?"

The cartoon ends with Rune alone in a tree, the moon spinning. Cryptic symbols light up the sky for a moment, transforming it. Rune closes his eyes and the screen goes dark. Tess stares at the screen, smiling as tears stream down her face.

Rain pounds against the window. Nicole chews her lip before she speaks. "OK, we don't have to talk about our parents. We don't have to dig all that stuff up. I get it. That's for therapy. That's fine. But Tess, just because I'm leaving tomorrow doesn't mean I don't care, OK? I promise I'll stay in touch, I won't disappear again. If I do that, can you promise me you're going to take care of yourself?" Tess doesn't reply, just keeps staring at the screen. "Tess, come on. It makes me really nervous hearing you talk like that. You sound like Mom with all that referential delusion type shit."

The next cartoon starts with a melancholy blues riff. A cloudy sky, dark wings, a farm. Chickens shimmy into a dilapidated barn for the night, and shortly after, Rune squeezes through a hole in the roof. The farmer from the first cartoon creeps across the acreage.

"It's not that I don't want to talk about Mom and Dad. I'd love to talk about them, but you always have such nasty things to say. They did everything they could for us. I miss them *so* much. Why are you always so mean?"

Nicole pauses, presses her lips together, but the words spill out anyway. "Because Mom was fucking crazy, Tess! Besides all the shit she did to us, and there was *plenty* of it, and that was bad enough, but besides that, she fucking *murdered* Dad and killed herself! And no one was surprised! Fuck, this hero worship is doing you no favors. You've got to process this shit if you don't want to end up like her."

Tess blinks, then her eyes creep back to the screen. Rune stares back at her. The farmer has cornered him in the barn. He reaches for something on the wall. "You know, the cartoonist of this died penniless. I don't know, did I read that somewhere, or do I just know it? Either way, it really fucks me up. You can see the occult vibes, right? Those weird symbols in the last cartoon, that whole creation schtick in the first one. Fuck, I don't know. It bothers me. I feel really weird. Does this sound crazy? I think I know what he was trying to do. He was trying to make Rune successful, like with those symbols, they meant something, but he forgot to make himself successful too, right, and so Rune ended up exploding in success but he didn't get any of it. What happens to that energy, do you think? That frustration and betrayal? Where does it go?"

The hand clenches a hammer. The hammer swings, flattens Rune, and for a moment there is silence. A moment to process the squished body, the bulging eyes, the spray of feathers, blood, and then Rune pops back up, unharmed. The magic of cartoons. Nicole opens her mouth, closes it again. A pause, then she huffs out a long breath. "I'm going to bed."

Tess' face collapses. "It's early. Come on, you didn't even eat any of the snacks I made." Nicole doesn't respond. Somber horns fill the room as she slinks out of it, shoulders slumped.

The end credits run. Tess' eyes never leave the screen as static fills it. She sinks to her knees on the floor, and inches closer to the TV, and when Rune returns she hears what he whispers and she says, "Yes."

***

Dawn brings a slim warm light into the living room. The couch envelops Tess. Blankets have sprouted up overnight, and the bookshelves loom in, making things feel tighter. Upstairs, Nicole's alarm, and then the sounds of her getting up, flushing the toilet, washing her face. Tess sinks deeper into the sofa. The cartoons blare louder, the music more frantic beneath crackling distortion.

"God, the air is so stuffy in here." Nicole has two suitcases in her hands, drops them by the door. "Are you still up? Did you go to bed at all?"

"Watchin' cartoons."

Nicole stops to look at the screen. Rune's eyes roll madly in his head, his claws expand and contract as he swoops down onto a rabbit. "Is this the same tape? You're watching it again?"

"Nope, different."

Nicole looks around the room. Old toys are strewn across the carpet. Books tumble from the bookshelves. "I thought we donated most of this stuff. Where did this all come from?" She picks up a stained stuffed animal with a frown. A bunny. An old hand-me-down, one of Nicole's favorites as a kid. "I definitely remember donating this." Tess' eyes don't move from the screen, and her thumb creeps into her mouth. Nicole shifts weight from one foot to the other. "I'm just going to make a quick coffee and then I've got to get going. Do you want anything?"

"Come sit with me."

"I've got to get going, Tess. You know that."

"Just watch one cartoon. This one is ending. Watch the next one with me."

"I don't have time for this." Nicole goes to the kitchen and the sound of her making coffee blends with the trumpet music as the next cartoon begins. When Nicole comes back to the room with her coffee, she looks more frazzled. Pale. "Did you paint the fucking kitchen overnight?"

Tess' eyes don't leave the screen.

"Why does everything look different? I don't get it." Her voice is thinner, near the edge of anxiety. She swallows her coffee and winces.

"Looks the same as it always did."

"You're freaking me out, Tess. I can't stay. I can't make you better, you have to look after yourself. I'm leaving. I don't care what weird shit you get up to."

"'Kay." Rune soars through the air, something moving in the dark pools of his eyes.

Nicole looks at the screen, then looks at Tess, thumb in her mouth, curled into the side of the couch. She checks the time and sighs, sits next to Tess. Takes her hand. "You're going to go to therapy later today, yeah? I'll call you when I land. You are important to me, even if it doesn't seem like it. But I have a life to get back to. I can't look after you forever. I've done everything I can. OK?"

Tess nods, but doesn't look away from the screen. Nicole waits a few seconds, sighs. "OK. I'm headed out then. I love you." She kisses Tess on the top of her head. Her soft hair smells like apple shampoo, the same cheap kind they both used as kids. Nicole frowns.

"I'll call you when I get in." Nicole leaves her coffee on the table. She picks up her suitcases with shaking hands and heads to the front porch. Tess snuggles deeper into the couch, clutching the stuffed bunny Nicole picked up earlier.

Rune dances with a group of barnyard animals, and one by one, takes them away into the woods, until only Rune is left, dancing. Tess watches and Rune smiles at her.

Nicole's curses interrupt the cheery music. Her face is red and puffy when she comes back into the living room. "What did you do to the door?"

"Didn't do nothin'."

"It won't open. I don't have time for this!" She storms to the back door and Rune opens his wings and rats fly out and Nicole comes back and now her face is really red. "What did you do?" She grabs Tess' arm, hard, and Tess shrugs her off and stares at the screen. "Why won't anything open? Fuck! I'll crawl out the window if I have to." Nicole rolls up her sleeves and moves towards the living room window.

"I'm gonna get some cereal." Tess wanders into the kitchen and pours a colorful bowl of sugar and marshmallows, adds milk, grabs a spoon. Nicole is cursing in the living room, but the music drowns her out. When Tess comes back, Nicole is crying. It's OK, though, because the cartoons are on and she can just sit and watch them, and everything else can fade into the distance.

Rune is flying over a row of cottages and the lights go off one by one, until he is just a dark shape moving in darkness, wings and talons and teeth and Nicole is saying something, and Nicole is angry, but Tess is safe. She is on the couch watching cartoons. She spoons more cereal into her mouth. Rune dances on screen, his wings wiggling in tune to the music. Symbols move in the expanse of darkness behind him. Tess laughs, she can't help it. Then Nicole is shaking her, and Tess' glassy eyes shift slowly to Nicole's pale face. "What did you do to my phone? What the fuck is going on here?" Nicole's breathing is fast. Sweat drips down her forehead. "I don't understand what's happening."

"I dunno. Why don't you just hang out with me? Do you want some cereal?"

"I don't want any fucking cereal," Nicole spits. She storms out of the room, through the kitchen, down into the basement. Tess slurps the last milk out of her bowl and takes her dishes to the kitchen to rinse. She pauses, listening to Nicole rustling around in the basement, then pours more cereal into her bowl. There's plenty. They'll never run out. When Nicole comes back up, there's a hammer in her hand. "Where the fuck did this come from, Tess? This shouldn't be here."

Tess shrugs.

"This is *it*, isn't it? Isn't it? The police should have this, this shouldn't be here. How did this get back here?"

Tess walks back into the living room. Nicole storms past her to the window. The flat thuds of the hammer against glass seem to frustrate her more, until she is screaming. "Why is it so dark out? Where is everything?" Nicole paces back and forth, her hair soaked with sweat. Tess closes her eyes, and time passes, so much time, the jazzy notes of the cartoon swell and fade and swell and fade, and eventually Nicole's sobs slow down, soften, and finally Tess wraps her arms around her and lowers her to the couch. She covers her with a blanket and they sink back into the cushions and the crying stops. Nicole lets herself be held and Tess shoves more cereal into her mouth and keeps her eyes on the TV.

***

"I can't do this anymore." Nicole is pacing again.

Tess doesn't mind. It's easy to ignore her. She's said it before, dozens of times, and yet they're still here, watching cartoons together. Rune scuttles up a tree and Tess giggles at the screen, greasy hair shadowing her face.

"It feels like we've been here forever." A cluster of zits near Nicole's mouth break open and ooze.

"We have. It's always like this. Just me and you watching cartoons. Come sit with me."

Nicole yanks at her hair, looks out the window again, into the swirling darkness. "I miss my cat. I miss my life. I was supposed to go home."

"This is your home. You're making me dizzy walking around like that." Tess puts her thumb in her mouth. "Come watch the cartoon."

Nicole screams. No words, just a shrill expression of rage. The hammer is in her hand again. It's heavy and makes her shoulder sag. "You did this, didn't you?" Tess doesn't say anything, puts her thumb in her mouth. Nicole takes a step closer, another. "*How* did you do this?" Tess shrugs.

Nicole raises the hammer.

Unlike the window, the TV crumples under the blow. The screen shatters. Tiny fragments of glass rip into Nicole's forearms. Blood dribbles onto the stained carpet as she swings the hammer again and again. Plastic crumples. The electronic insides hiss and fizzle.

The television is dead.

Nicole falls to her knees.

Silence fills the room, broken only by the wet sounds of Tess sucking her thumb.

A hum of static.

The TV puts itself back together in fits and starts. The air in the room feels heavier, more difficult to breathe. The glass flies back into shape, a groan and hum of wires, and Nicole is screaming but she tires herself out quickly, because by the time her voice grows hoarse the cartoons are back on. Tess reaches for her sister, touches her sticky hair, but Nicole shrugs her off.

"You did this, didn't you?"

"Mmm." Rune devours a mouse, claws and talons ripping it to shreds, and the mouse's skeleton hops up and does a little jig.

Nicole's breathing is thin. "I love you but I'm not staying. I've got to stop this somehow. I'm not staying. Not here."

She picks up the hammer again.

It comes down hard against Tess' temple. The bone crumples, the flesh caves. Nicole grunts, and something flickers across her face. Tess doesn't move, just smiles faintly, and the hammer smashes into her nose this time. A gush of blood, a spray of bone. Her eye bulges under the pressure, weeps red tears. The hammer flies again and again and again until Tess' face is just a smear of red on the couch, and Nicole screams but the doors still won't open, and the window still won't budge, and the red fades to black and white, and there is a groan and a wheeze as Tess' face bounces back, a crunch as her features fill back in, and she looks younger somehow, even younger than before, and on the screen, Rune is pacing back and forth and he really is such a funny character, the way his limbs change shape as they move. The cartoonists didn't have a plan in mind when they made those original cartoons, it was just raw sweat and blood and ink, and it was amazing what they could create, or what they could discover, and the little creatures move across the screen and they dance and finally Nicole laughs and the jazz is suffocating and this time when Tess asks her if she wants some cereal she says yes and settles deeper into the couch.

JOHN LIST WOULD LIKE TO CANCEL HIS SUBSCRIPTION TO OMAHA STEAKS

Rae Knowles

"THAT'S RIGHT, a family vacation," John said, lowering his hand from the dial. As the AC kicked on, he cringed. Sixty degrees would be unthinkable under any other circumstance. Who would ever need a home that cold? The bill would be outrageous.

The whirr of a nearby vent obscured the voice of the receptionist on the other end, but he thought he made out something like *winter breaks* and *make-up assignments*.

"Thank you, ma'am."

"Of course, Mr. List. Enjoy your holiday."

The tangled cord spun and wrapped around itself as he placed the phone in its proper resting place. From the mantle, a portrait leered. He pulled the notepad from his pocket, drawing a single line through *Call the school* and tucked it safely inside his coat, the next item, *Photos*, top of mind.

John took a high step to reach his duffle bag, avoiding the soiled carpet. Slinging the strap over one arm and sliding open the zipper, he ushered the portrait inside. Making his way from room to room, collecting images of himself as he went, it struck him that every picture captured the same vacant expression. A bit winded when he climbed to the second floor, he was suddenly relieved to feel the icy breath of the air conditioning on the back of his neck.

Good planning, John, he assured himself.

A void in his stomach grumbled. The bank had taken longer than expected, he'd had to stop at the field, and then the whole mess with his eldest boy . . . His shoulder ached in the socket. John was not the young man he once was. He stretched his arm from one side to the other. Had he dislocated it? It didn't matter. He had a plan.

And dinner was thirty minutes past due.

Making his way through the children's rooms and back down the stairs, he hoped Helen hadn't eaten all the ham, that Alma had secured the twist tie on the bread so it wasn't stale, *again*. Framed photos clanked against one another in the duffle, but he knew the cash beneath would provide enough cushion to keep the glass from breaking, and when he reached the kitchen, he lowered the bag onto Patricia's empty chair.

There were a few slices of ham left. The bread was only partially stale, and as John munched the sandwich, he once again checked over his list.

Omaha Steaks.

The next delivery was due a week from Sunday, two New York strips and a porterhouse. He couldn't have them rotting on the porch. The kitchen phone had an extra long cord, and though he usually thought it was gauche, John set the receiver face up on the table and placed the call on speaker so he could finish his lunch and remain, for the most part, on schedule.

She answered on the second ring.

"Omaha Steaks, delivering premium meats since 1917. How might I help you?"

"Hello, this is Mr. List and I'm calling to cancel my subscription."

"Oh!" Her voice lost none of its cheeriness. "I am so sorry to hear, Mr. List. Was the last delivery," clicking in the background, "on September 21st not to your satisfaction?"

"It's not that." John moved a bite of ham, smothered in a too large bead of mayo, to the back of his mouth. "We're going out of town, you see."

"How lovely. A trip for the holidays?"

"Yes." John sucked down a swallow of milk. "The whole family will be gone, so there will be no one here to receive the package." His eyes wandered over the center of the ballroom. "I hate to think of it rotting."

"Well, Mr. List, I can put your mind at ease. No need to cancel, we can delay the delivery. When do you expect to return?"

"That's the thing—" John cleared his throat, mucous already flaring up from the dairy. "We're moving."

A beat passed.

"After your vacation?"

"After our vacation." John stood and rinsed the empty glass under the faucet. Noticing a rusty smudge at his wrist, he wiped it away with the excess moisture. It must have hid beneath his cuff, but there was no excuse for sloppiness. John would need to be more careful.

"Moving is quite the undertaking, Mr. List. Wouldn't it be nice to have one less thing to worry about while you're unpacking boxes? We can transfer your subscription, if you give us the new address, I can update our system and change the delivery date—"

She was talking fast now, customer service training no doubt kicking in, so John had to cut her off. "I'm not interested, thank you."

"Perhaps you'd like to check with your wife?" More clicking keys. "Won't the kids miss steak dinners? We have you down as a family of five."

"Six." John let the ire shoot through him and waft away. "My mother has a room in the attic."

"How good of you, John, taking care of your mother. May I call you John?"

John shifted. He hadn't expected the flush of warmth in her tone. "Sure."

"Well, John, would you like to check with them before we cancel? Just to be sure?"

Again, John's eyes passed over the ballroom. "There's no need."

"I understand. I'm going to go ahead and transfer you to my supervisor to complete the cancellation. Hold please."

A cheesy instrumental version of an Eagles song—John couldn't remember which one—gave him an idea. While he waited, he went to the radio in the ballroom, setting it to play an AM Christian station at full volume.

" . . . *crouched, waiting to steal, lie, and devour.*"

"John List?" This voice had syrupy notes of southern sweetness.

"*Damnation awaits those who stray from the path . . .*"

"Yes!" he called over the recorded sermon, scuttling back from the neighboring room.

" . . . *Mercy shall be saved for those deemed righteous.*"

"My colleague tells me you'd like to cancel your subscription."

John cradled the phone using his body, his best attempt to block the background noise. He cleared his throat. "That's right."

"She says you and your *whole* family are going away, and then moving." John couldn't place the strange inflection on the word.

So, he just said, "That's right."

"You know," the woman let her breath crackle over the line, "sometimes I get calls from men who think they want to cancel their order."

"*. . . to inherit the kingdom of God . . .*"

Light refracted off the gun's barrel. He'd laid it there, still hot, and now the evening sun seemed to wink at him as it poured through the blinds and bounced off the black metal.

"But they really just want to reduce the quantity. Say . . . from family of five—six, you said! To just one."

"*Abraham so trusted in the Lord . . .*"

John mindlessly rubbed his fingertips together where the burn interrupted his usual swirl pattern. "Just one." He'd been too quick to pick up the spent casing.

"*Faith! Pure faith!*"

"Our cuts are the highest quality," she continued, "but our New York strips are nearly a pound, our porterhouses more like a pound and a half. That's a lot of meat, John. Don't you think?"

John's thought, *too much, too heavy,* came out as a *hmmm.*

"You're not the only one. So many men think they want a family portion, think they *should be able to handle* that much meat. But it's too much sometimes, isn't it, John?"

John let the silence hang there as he considered it. Hard as he tried, it had been too much.

"Good men, capable providers, even . . . "

She continued but John could only focus on the scent of iron, the relentless nagging, the beast that was sin moving ever closer to his children, his legacy, the threat that crescendoed into a scheduled series of blasts, and now the quiet—the delicious quiet made thicker by the hum of the AC.

"So, do you?"

A flush of embarrassment. John was meticulous; he didn't like missing things. He didn't like repeating things. A flash of his eldest boy, grunting, uniform stained. "Do I what?"

"Do you think reducing your order, rather than canceling it, might be the way to go?"

When was the last time John enjoyed a steak? *Really* enjoyed it, without the press of eyes across the table?

"As I said, we can change the delivery address. Maybe somewhere out west? It's really no trouble at all."

"Out west?" John had a vague idea of where he would go, but wanted to hear out this woman, this woman who seemed to understand him more than Helen, certainly more than Alma or the kids.

"I hear lovely things about Denver. We can hold your order 'til you're settled in there. You can just give me a call back. Wendy. You call and ask for Wendy."

"That's kind of you, Wendy." When was the last time a woman had taken the time to be kind to him?

"The cold is important, John."

A shiver crept over his shoulder blades. "The cold?"

"Our meat is stored in a deep freezer to ensure freshness. Without the cold, it would really be a mess."

John smirked. He let his gaze pass over the windows: firmly shut, blinds closed. He let his mind wander and find the image of rotted meat, a green, iridescent sheen around clusters of pearl-sized eggs, maggots nestling into layers of rancid tissue, making a home there. Then he thought of clean cuts, frozen and meticulously packaged so not a drop of blood leaked through, the blue hue of freezer lighting, the neat, chilled stack in the ballroom. "Yes, the cold is important."

"Very important."

John eyed the duffle bag, the duffle bag containing his fresh start.

"It's a long trip to Denver."

An undisturbed steak did sound nice, a steak alone in Denver.

"You know what I'd like to do for you, John?"

"What's that?"

"I'd like to open you a new account, for *just one* under a new name. Something that will blend in Denver—or anywhere, really. Something like Bob . . . Bob Clark. What do you say?"

"Bob Clark." John had thought of Roger Hammons, but this was even better, less remarkable. "It's a strong name."

"Oh yes." More clicking. "A strong name for a man strong enough to start over, and not cheat himself out of the finer things in the process. Are two weeks enough?"

"Are two weeks enough for what?"

"To settle in Denver. I'll schedule you for a call back in two weeks, Mr. Clark."

It was silly.

John knew that.

She didn't want to lose a customer, likely worked on commission. She didn't know. She had no special affection toward him, but still . . . the way she rolled Mr. Clark off her tongue . . . For the first time in a long time, John felt less alone.

"How will you get my number?"

"Hah!" A light smack of flesh on flesh, and John pictured the woman slapping her forehead. "Of course, how silly of me. You'll call me then. This number is just fine, you can ask for Wendy."

"Yeah, you said that."

"Do we have a plan, Mr. Clark?"

John pulled a ballpoint pen from the kitchen junk drawer. "It's a plan."

"Excellent, Bob. I look forward to speaking with you soon." A gentle click and John walked the phone back to its resting place on the wall. Once more, he pulled the notebook from his pocket, this time penning a new entry.

November 23, call Omaha Steaks: Wendy

Below, he scrawled the customer service number.

John pushed the crumbs from his plate into the sink drain and rinsed the dish, drying his palms on the hand towel. Lifting the gun from the counter, he switched the safety on and tucked it into the duffle bag still resting on Patricia's empty chair.

Stepping over the heap of bodies in the ballroom, John took one last look at his massive home, running through the list.

Bank. Check.

Gas. Check.

Cancel milk, mail, newspaper. Check.

Pastor's letter. Check.

Lights on. Close blinds. Check.

Turn down AC. Check.

Call the school. Check.

Photos. Check.

Omaha Steaks. Check.

Turning up each foot, he examined the soles of his shoes—no blood. With a sigh, he let himself out, locking the door behind him. Duffle bag secured in the trunk, John—*No*, he reminded himself, *Bob*— flipped the ignition, and set course west. To Denver.

Where a quiet steak dinner was waiting.

THERE ARE WITCHES IN THE WOODS.

These are the words the reverend of the Lilin Assembly of Our Lord repeats to his parishioners each week. Steve and Nicole Warby think it's just a metaphor, until Nicole takes a walk in those woods and comes back changed. Something came out of them with her, and the simple small-town life they've always known is forever altered when they discover the dark secrets buried deep and those intent on keeping them there. Fearing for his wife's sanity, and his own comfortable status in the church, Steve is unsure if he wants to help or ignore the problems. The reverend believes there are witches in the woods, and he thinks Nicole is only the most recent.

AVAILABLE NOW!
WWW.GHOULISHBOOKS.COM

GOOP BY GOOP
The INs and outs of Shunting

Lor Gislason

IF YOU'VE NEVER seen *Society*—what are you doing here? Go watch it.

Okay, now we can get down to business. *Society* is the big daddy of mushy, melty body horror with the iconic SHUNTING scene, and I love it more than a sane person should. From the second the film starts, we're teased as it plays out of focus behind the credits. When the reveal finally drops . . . it's just magnificent. Giant hands for heads, backward feet, ripping bodies apart all while the Socialities moan and clearly enjoy themselves. Just a big ol' goopy orgy. So how did this scene come about? What went into these effects that still hold a permanent space in my brain years later?

Society is the baby of Brian Yuzna. He got his start as a producer for his buddy Stuart Gordan, lending a hand to *Re-Animator, From Beyond* and *Dolls,* then making the move to behind the camera. *Re-Animator* did particularly well, guaranteeing a sequel—which Yuzna owned the rights to. Gordon didn't really want to direct. Yuzna told the studio, "Fine, I'll direct *Bride of Re-Animator,* but first, you have to let me make this weird cult movie so I can get some work experience, and also not feel too bad if it's a diaster." "Ya sure, OK," they said, clearly not expecting what became *Society*. It's Yuzna's directorial debut, which to me is amazing. Where do you go from here? You've already created a masterpiece. You're horror Da Vinci.

"Even if I totally screwed up (making *Society*)

on my first [film], I'm still guaranteed one more chance!" I love this outlook. Sucking at something is the first step to getting good, a wise dog once said.

Thankfully, the blood cult aspects were changed to weird, high-society aliens, and the entire film was built around big special effects scenes, with character development sprinkled here and there. "If I'm gunna make a movie, I want some weird stuff!" Yuzna said. Words to live by.

Another legend joins the crew. *Surrealistic Makeup Effects by Screaming Mad George* is definitely the raddest opening credit in movie history. You know you're in for a good time when that pops up. Real name Joji Tani, this mad lad was suggested by the film's Japanese producers. Bringing his experience from *Nightmare on Elm Street 3 & 4,* the latter of which includes the horrible cockroach scene (one of the few *NoES* deaths where I feel legit bad for the character) and an almost excessive, Frank rising from the dead in *Hellraiser-level* of slime, George was perfect for the job.

The plot, which can be best described as "Billy's no good very awful week"—turns out his rich family adopted him fully intending to chow down on him later. Several of his friends go missing, and no one takes Billy seriously, especially his psychiatrist. This culminates with him sneaking into what is outwardly a coming out party for his sister, but in reality, a bunch of rich people eating his friend, aka THE SHUNTING. And yes I keep repeating it because frankly, it's fun to say.

So once everyone strips down to their skivvies, they start "shunting", basically melting and combining, including all over Billy's friend

Blanchard. He's the first course. They rip open his stomach, pluck off his mole like a piece of chocolate, and while the others hold him down, the comical cigar-smoking mayor shoves his fist up Blanchard's asshole till it bursts out of his mouth. Also one of them is recording it—what, are they going to watch it later like home movies?

The designs for the Shunting creatures were based on Yuzna's nightmares and several Salvador Dali paintings, including one called *Soft Construction with Boiled Beans (Premonition of Civil War)*, very catchy I must admit, and another which speaks for itself: *The Great Masturbator*. And at least for Yuzna, he seemed to have the time of his life, describing it as *"audacious and thrilling"* in an interview with Fangoria.

"I got to do whatever I wanted to do, because when you're working with people on a low level like that, nobody tells you what to do. You do whatever you want!" He told Neon Zombie. "I knew my friends were gunna see this movie and go, 'who let you do that!?' cuz everybody would always complain about producers, they don't let them shoot what they want, but for me, I never had that problem. I felt like, any time I had a chance to make a movie, that was good."

The morphing, jiggly people are meant to induce paranoia, shifting in shape when you look away, but they never get too serious about it, which is something that I think sets the film apart from "am I crazy or is everyone crazy". It's *funny*. You understand what you're seeing is horrifying—a father and mother having a weird sexual relationship with their daughter—but then she walks around like Cotton Hill with huge Hobbit feet, and Billy's dad has his face coming out of a butt. "I guess I am a butthead!" Incredible.

"I remember the orgy scene quite well." Billy Warlock, who you'll never guess what role he played, recounted; "To this day I have never seen a group of people, from background artists who were filling in, to random extras, where everyone melded into everyone else with so much gusto. They were all just so into it and digging what they were doing. Mr. Slack (Billy's psychiatrist in the film) and those guys were having so much fun during that last sequence." That's dedication to the craft right there.

A dozen crew members were used to work the large, contorted puppet for the 'shunting' finale. It was moved from beneath the stage floor where the crew members were concealed, creating a swiss cheese obstacle course for actors to work on. If they missed a mark, they'd fall—which was even more likely considering everything was doused in an extremely slippery food-thickening gel. I wonder if they just hosed everyone down at the end of the day.

It's impressive that they accomplished all of this for only a million dollars. When the film debuted in London, it was called "stupid yet brilliant" which is the highest compliment I could imagine receiving. Unfortunately, it was shelved for three years in the US, seemingly because Americans took it too seriously. "While the Brits may go ballistic over the notion that their class-heavy society is indeed a plot against the everyman, here in the States we tend to be more wary of the electorate than the greed-mongers who finance them," wrote Mark Savlov of the Austin Chronicle. Another possibility is due to Billy Warlock being on *Baywatch* around the same time, which was massively popular—and audiences just didn't want to see this hot dude getting gooped on.

Thankfully it joined the long line of horror films that gain traction on VHS. I myself watched it on tape, rented from the local Mom & Pop rental place as a teenager. And now thanks to the internet, it's widely available if you know where to look.

Overall, it's the combination of going full bore with a ridiculous idea, dream logic and "wow that looks cool" attitude that gives *Society* a specific place in horror history. It's not as popular as *The Thing* or other effects heavy, melty films, but it's perfect for horny weirdos like me.

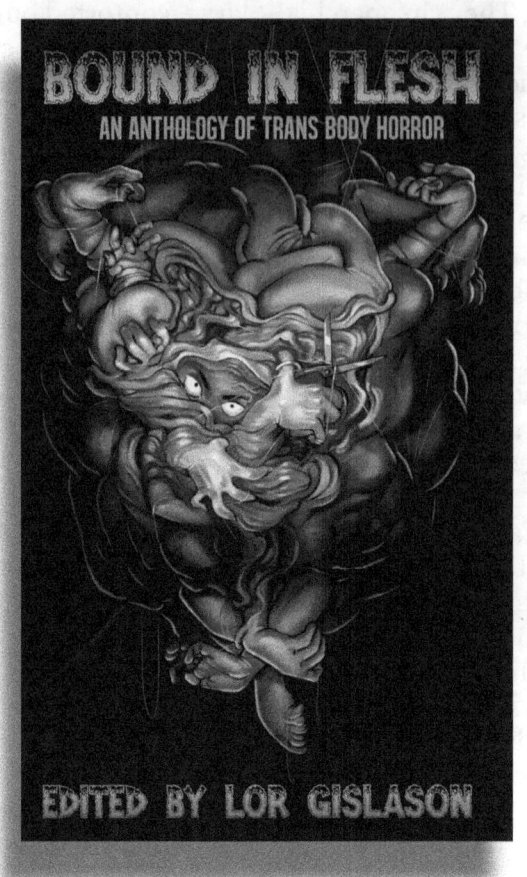

TONIGHT'S GUEST IS!

Robert Nazar Arjoyan

HE NEEDED SOMEONE to turn the heater down, for God's sake, there were already sweats pooling under his pits. As much as he loved doing the talk shows, he hated the green rooms. But Joe Bach didn't complain. The life he led was lucky.

He would call out, perfectly certain someone would come because someone always did. Those in earshot could actually *hear* his smile. It was a power he'd always had and used.

Joe cleared his throat once and let loose the award winner, the crowd pleaser, the sea parter.

"Excuse me?" rang the avuncular voice recognized in every developed country—most of the third world for that matter. And if for some reason his voice went unidentified, then his face would be a dead giveaway. His lapis lazuli eyes, the free fall of his snowing hair, a wrinkle in the right corner of his mouth.

Joe Bach had grown up with one generation, fathered another, and now bounced their successors on both of his knees. Everyone had a favorite Joe Bach movie and anyone charmed enough to have met the man himself walked away feeling lighter, better, happier.

"Yes, Mr. Bach?" A PA's head popped in.

"Joe, please. No 'mister' anything," beamed Joe. He knew how to make anyone feel comfortable in his presence and really, he was at ease with folks of all kinds.

"Could we turn the heater down a tad, please?" continued Joe. "I would myself but I couldn't seem to find a console or station or whatever they're called." Joe chuckled as the PA consulted her iPad.

"I believe your people told us that you like it a little warmer than usual?"

"Warm, sure, but it's a bit too warm just now."

"Copy that. We'll turn it down right away."

"Thank you so much. What's your name?"

"Marina."

"Thank you so much, Marina. I appreciate it."

See? The world could function properly with just a sprinkling of kindness. Knowing someone's name, saying please and thank you, lookin em in the eye. Status is nice, Joe wasn't a fool, but at the end of the day, he was a person just like Marina.

Joe relaxed and got ready for the hot seat.

***

"Five minutes, Mr. Bach."

Joe opened his eyes and saw Marina at the door. He spotted lights prancing behind her.

It took a long second to get his bearings. Who was the host again? They all bled into each other after a while. He was here to plug his new . . . movie? No, it was the memoir!

Was it time to write one of those already? An obligatory obituary written, edited, and proofed by any celebrity worth their salt. No ghostwriter for Joe Bach.

Joe stood and stretched. The one action movie he tried in the 90s left him with a shattered knee and it smarted more than ever. He winced at the sudden buckling and fell on the crafts table. The turkey slices his team requested were ham. The chocolate chip cookies he loved were oatmeal raisin. Such blatant erring pissed Joe off, if he was being honest, but after a deep breath and a short talking-to, he realized it was the bum knee just exacerbating things. Ham reminded Joe of Christmas, his favorite holiday, while the oatmeal cookies painted a pretty picture of Jess.

He grabbed one and bit. Joe stopped mid-chew. He ground his jaw and teeth slowly.

"I'll be damned," he muttered. Joe would've sworn on a stack of Bibles that these cookies tasted just like—no, were indeed his grandgirl's. He pocketed another, thinking already how to bring it up on camera. Everyone would eat that up.

He laughed inwardly.

Tie straight, hair just so, cookie in pocket, Joe went to greet his adoring public. And anyway, he was all too ready to leave this blasted furnace.

Someone had turned the heater on again.

***

The curtain was crimson and crushed. Joe waited for his cue as he'd waited countless times before. Surefooted and never nervy.

"Ready?" It was Marina again.

Joe understood intellectually that she was just doing her job but, come on. *Ready?* Joe didn't like the cut of her gib.

"Yup," he assured.

"Our second guest canceled, unfortunately, so you'll have to fill in both slots."

"Ah," scoffed Joe. "No problemo!"

"Do you have stuff you can talk about?"

Joe was certain that she was just trying to get his goat. One of those kids who ironically didn't like him, who thought him disingenuous and his acting canned.

Well, fuck her.

"I have stuff I can talk about, yes."

"Good. We're back in thirty."

She loped away, whispering in someone's ear who'd whisper it to someone else and so on and so forth until the message would unquestionably become *Joe Bach has warts on his toes.*

Would he get paid for the overtime? He was certain his agent would take care of that after the fact. Other than the action movie snag, she was a winner in Joe's eyes. Took care of all his needs. Nell earned every bit of her ten percent.

The live band kicked into high gear and the audience applauded, whooping and hollering.

Joe heard a husky voice slither out of the speakers.

"Welcome back to *Tonight's Guest Is*! We're very fortunate this evening to have with us a paragon of cinema, a model human being, and everyone's favorite man. He's someone's father, he's someone's son, he's Joe Bach! Give it up, kids!"

The curtains came to life and swung apart. The powerful lights hit Joe with a blinding force and he put a hand up to shield his eyes from the rays. They should've done a walkthrough earlier in the day. Why hadn't that been arranged? Whatever—a set is a set is a set.

Joe had walked over them all.

The man behind the desk was smaller than Joe but swarthier—deep tan, black hair and brows, and a most impeccably shaven face. Joe respected anyone who knew how to shave correctly. The host was smiling and cajoling him onward with waves and *clapter*. One of Joe's secrets was this word, a portmanteau of clap and laughter. It sounded more natural to him than *applause*.

"Joe Bach, everyone! Let's hear it!"

The mirth of the crowd rose to a roar. Swept up by the pandemonium, Joe hooted back. Again, he could be comfortable with the President of the United States or strangers in a bar. What's more, Joe loved this shit. He made like it was nothing, but it got him hard in all the places that mattered.

He took a bow and sat beside his host. But oh hell, Joe didn't know this guy's name! Wouldn't do to start the program by asking this fella's name, not at all. He racked his prodigious memory, certain the handle was nestled in there someplace. He could of course employ his seldom seen improv chops and make a—

"Joe, Abe Lyon. Been waiting a long time to meet you!"

"Well, Abe, that's kind of you and I'm glad to be your guest."

To underscore the general bonhomie fomenting betwixt Abe and Joe, the crowd broke into another round of ovation.

"Ah, clapter," declared Abe. "Keeps this show on the air!"

The wrinkle curving around Joe's mouth deepened. Did this Abe just say clapter? Could be a . . . coincidence, of course, people make up words like that all the time-

"And a nice segue right into the memoir, I'd

say. Aren't I doing good so far, Joe?" The lights were glaring, sparkling, intense. And quite hot.

It made seeing any part of the spectators impossible.

"The memoir, you said?"

"Yes, your memoir!" Joe noticed that this man spoke in exclamations strictly. From beneath his desk, Abe pulled out a hardcover copy of Joe's book.

"*Someone's Father, Someone's Son.* What an exquisite title."

"Heh, thanks, thank you very much." Joe's editor, Carl, came up with the title. Nell made Carl sign an NDA stipulating that he'd never reveal this information.

"Kudos to your editor for such an inspired choice, eh?"

Joe's head snapped back but Abe kept on rambling and wouldn't let Joe get a word in.

"It's a doorstop, this thing, look at it! You, zoom in with camera B. What a monster, huh?"

As Abe held the book up, Joe thought it looked . . . thicker.

"I have forever been a devourer of people's lives and this book is delicious."

"I'm sorry, is that a new edition?"

Abe turned the book over in his hirsute hand, inspecting it.

"Don't think so!" He perused the copyright page, his filed nail denting the folio.

"By the way, Joe, this dedication: 'for my Jess.' That's your granddaughter, right?"

The cookie! A better lead-in couldn't have been written.

"That's right, Abe. In fact, the funniest thing happened."

"Tell!"

"In the green room today, everything was off! Turkey was ham, water was wine, and chocolate chip cookies were oatmeal raisin. You guys did not have that room together."

Joe chuckled to reassure everything was fine, just fine.

"But when I tasted it, the cookie, I mean, I would have taken an oath that it was from a batch of Jess's. So I rationed another for later."

Now, thought Joe, I will reach into my pocket and seal the d—

"Ahhh!" Joe shot up out of his chair.

"Joe, Joe! What happened? Are you alright?"

Joe took his jacket off like a man on fire and tossed it away.

"There was something in my pocket! I took a cookie from the green room and I'd planned to eat it . . . but . . . I don't know what but something just touched me!"

The audience grumbled, some giggled.

"Why don't we go to commercial? I won't let you go anywhere!" Abe flashed a grin and kept it until the all-clear. Then his face drooped.

"Joe, are you OK?"

"I'm telling you, man, there was something in my pocket."

"Let's take a looksee."

"Go for it. I'm waiting here."

Abe walked over to the blazer and Joe noticed the man wasn't wearing shoes.

His feet were bare.

Abe reached into the offending pocket and after feeling around, produced the cookie.

"Whatever it was must have crawled away," conjectured Joe.

"Possible. These are very old studios."

From the wings: "Back in thirty."

"Come on, Joe, let's really get into it now. Do you want the cookie?"

Joe just shook his head. Later, the sight of Abe biting into the cookie would chill Joe perpetually.

"Let's talk about the book," suggested Joe.

"That's why we're here!"

Prompted by the winking sign above their heads, the studio audience ushered the cameras in with shouts and whistles.

"And we're back, my dears and acolytes! Sitting here with Joe Bach. Joe, we were just getting into the meat of your memoir. Dedicated to your granddaughter Jess, titled by your editor—"

"Really, no, we both batted around—"

"And still selling like hotcakes."

"I've been very fortunate."

A pause. Abe looked at Joe from down his sharp nose.

"And . . . I just felt like getting it all down and thanking the folks who helped me along the way." Joe nodded, swallowed. Threw his hands up and smiled.

"What a gent, this guy. Another round of clapter for our Joe!"

"Wait, wait. Stop. I'm—I'm just curious. You said it before and—"

"Said what?"

"Clapter. Where'd that come from?"

Abe made a goofy face.

"Ummm, your book, Joe."

Joe's heart picked up its pace.

"That's not in my book, Abe."

"Joe, I read this thing backwards and forwards."

"Yeah, and I wrote it." Joe's voice did what it did when he played Macbeth at the National.

Abe flipped through *Someone's Father, Someone's Son.*

"Aha. May I? 'The girl's vocabulary was nowhere near as fully fleshed as she. Before I actually had her—or any of them—I took time to make her feel cozy, snug, warm.'"

"Stop," commanded Joe. Abe did not heed.

"'We'd play a game or two, talk about movies, what they were learning in school. And this particular child—"

Joe wrenched the book from Abe.

"What the fuck do you think this is, huh? I will sue you and your entire—"

From under his desk, Abe brought out another copy of the book and picked up where he left off.

"And this particular child whose name I never learned—"

Joe snatched this one too but it, in turn, snatched him. America's actor began to elocute.

"'—because I never learned any of their names, asked me what it was like to hear clapter all the time. The unnamed and unnumbered and unflowered girl gave me this lovely word. She had a strange blemish on her left shoulder. I wish the others were gentler sometimes.'"

Joe stared at words he'd never written.

Only lived.

"Beautiful, Joe. Just beautiful! That entire chapter. And while it only spans one hundred pages, it was your entire life, wasn't it?"

If Joe was looking at his host, he'd have seen smoke drifting from Abe's mouth.

"Can we . . . can we lower the lights, please? It's incredibly hot."

"Those aren't the lights," was all Abe said.

Joe was sweating now and the smell of rotten eggs began to perforate from all around him.

"Writing is a basin in which to wash away one's sins. Those sins scamper and surge down the drain all the way to yours truly."

Joe looked at Abe now and saw him in truth.

"Marina, would you bring Joe here the surprise, please?"

Joe bolted for the curtain. It opened at his approach but he skidded to a halt. A naked little girl was pushing a cart laden with awards of gold and silver and bronze.

There was a ruddy discoloration on her shoulder.

"Marina?"

The child that Joe violated thirty years ago nudged past him.

"Guessed right, Joe. First prize! Add it to the heap, boys."

From an inky ceiling that was nothing but dripping stalactites fell another award.

"Good for you, Joe! We've already issued a press release to the mourning world via Nell. I like her, Joe, and I think she'll be joining us sooner than later. Come on, let's have another round of clapter!"

Clapter there was and louder it got. The throng stood. The gauze holding Joe's mind in place tore away when he saw the audience descend and approach.

Kids, all.

Innocents who were someone's son, someone's daughter, but never anyone's father, never anyone's mother. Marina dumped the cart into a chasm which had materialized out of nowhere. Great, steaming magma roiled and screamed, melting the history of Joe's victorious life.

The children came nearer to him.

"Careful, kids, this man is a danger to us all," warned Abe. Joe rotated his head and glanced at Abe, a red thing with red talons and a red penis. It hurt Joe's wilting eyes to look for long so he turned his blank stare to the children. There he found fury.

Abe—real name unsayable but sometimes called Apollyon—inserted a cloven hand into the maw of fire. From this cauldron a blade he hoisted, alloyed together from the muck of Joe's false narratives.

"Get him."

Leashed by the commands of domineering

adults, the children seized Joe with unrelenting and immovable loathing. He searched their faces, skimming from one unfamiliar visage to the next, never stopping.

As Abe scuffed his hooves toward Joe, erect and armed, the man loved by all, the man who loved all, had still one greater thing to fear: when would he spot Jess?

LEGERDEMAIN

Barbara Castro-Rojas

THERE'S A HOLE in the ground where it keeps.

Off the main road, past the roaring interstate. Jackie thought of nothing else on days when she was planning on visiting the hole. This thing that needed her. That she had created. It'd been too long since . . . *It's okay. It can't die in three days. It won't. Hurry up, Jackie. No time to waste.* She got there fast by walking under the old east pass, through the narrow tunnel which terrified her. This is the kind of place girls walk into and get killed, or worse, she thought. Too many stories and none of them happened to her yet. Six years back home and all she had to show for it was a failed affair and a job as a kid's dance instructor. And the last three days where it all came crashing down. Jackie sped up, ran, stood, looked, listened. A soft growling, a cat's purr, echoed back from the hole. Detritus formed a wet ring around the vantablack cavity. It was growing larger. She pulled up her sweater, exhaled.

I know you're hungry. I'm sorry. So sorry. Can never do anything right.

***

A tightening wind slapped against her belly. A mouthful of sweater, she pulled out a blade and started cutting. A small square on the lower side. Precise, given the blue light in the woods and her angle. A little more. She helped the unyielding peel of skin tear with a swerve of the blade—how easy it was to take off this flesh. She stuck the bit into her mouth. Over the past few months, it was getting easier not to gag. Her back hunched over the hole, catlike. Jackie masticated herself again. The blood pushed against the roof of her mouth, sloshing around the gummy bits. The dark cavity seemed to wait—an unnatural, patient quiet. She spit out the chewed-up meat into the hole. Bullseye. Her brother was wrong. She spits like the best of them: baseball player level. If they could see her now. A trickle of blood and saliva followed. Something in the hole rustled about. A sniff, hesitation, then wet, sucking noises. It ate greedily. Jackie leaned back and licked the salty sweat off her upper lip; a pleased grin on her face.

Not a chance she'd wait this long to come back. Besides, the hole was growing. Hungry. She drowned the open wound in alcohol and quickly wrapped her stomach in gauze. This wasn't the largest chunk she'd ever taken but the tender flesh of her belly made her wince. *I'm a miserable fragile thing but I can do this. Can they?* The back of her hair felt hot and she turned to face the last rays of daylight. Immediately, the bandage took a crimson color.

The dread returned as soon as she stepped foot in the house. A New Jersey two-story home with creaky floors and outdated heaters. Her father was watching television in his robe, as usual, and her mother was folding laundry. *Lint and drool, that's all we are.* She caught herself. *Honest people, with a shameful daughter,* she confessed. She pulled out her phone to confirm there were no new messages. The phone stared back blankly. Of course not.

That night, Jackie slept in her bed unshowered. The stickiness of her fingers helped pull the pages of the yearbook apart quite easily. She stared at the group photos of herself at the prom. Then moved to the photo albums. A young Jackie with a friend she no longer spoke to (she couldn't tell you the reason). A young Jackie at a company trip, where she'd gotten so drunk they asked her to leave early. A young Jackie at her brother's funeral, too involved in a breakup to remember the service. Selfish, stupid, coward. The three words she repeated—condemned—while brushing her teeth. But she kept looking at this face through time. Smeared her dirty fingers over the smiling fool of a girl she wanted to wipe away with the day's grime. So very badly. Every awkward conversation or memory flooded back to her in an instant. College was no different. The last few years, the same. A young woman at a bar, a married man. What a cliche. She buried her head into the pillow and screamed. Screamed so hard the wound throbbed with fresh blood and pain. In front of the hole, she was different. She was not selfish, stupid, or cowardly. She was self-sacrificing, smart, and brave.

Is tonight too soon to go back? A swarm of butterflies filled her stomach. First date jitters. She stared up at the ceiling for a moment. The fan droned in circles like her thoughts, each one driving another into her mind before any could take root. It kept going like that for some time. Tossing, turning, the night deepening. She made the decision on a whim. Her life motto. It started with needing to pee, then Jackie was out the door. When she got to the patch of forest, there was no hole anymore. It was more of a crater. Where are you? The forest leaves around the cavity had dissolved overnight, swallowed by the hole. Without thinking, she dropped her hand in. *If it takes my hand, so be it. Then I'll be reborn. New. No one will remember that immature girl from the yearbook.* Seconds later, her hand didn't find darkness or the hole's eager mouth. She hit against it again, hard, until the hollow pang of glass came back. It was a wall. Man-made. *What is this?* Her eyes widened. *How did it get here?* A familiar sense of dread, of shame. There was no time for thinking about all that. She kept digging out dead leaves and dirt, tiny bones that looked like rats. And the smell, the smell of it made her gag. Jackie didn't know what the dead smelled like, but she imagined it was something like this foul odor

burning her nose. Sewage, rotten eggs, primordial. She kept going until the wall thing was visible. Until she was . . . vertical. She grabbed whatever she could find in the earth, branches, bones. *I'm falling. God, I'm falling.* She opened her eyes. No, the earth was vertical now. And the glass wall was farther away in this strange cave. In she walked. *Thing? Where are you?* Her wounds hurt, old and new. The stomach, the tip of her right pinky, the lip of her crotch, the soft flesh near her shoulder.

Jackie, said a voice.

Then . . .

Jackie? Jackie?!

There it was: hobbled and rising to the light from her hole. It looked like her and not like her. From where she stood, the skin looked partly flayed. A patchwork of pink and white peels with creases of gray hair. Rat skins. The figure stood, watching her, then walked closer. It was shorter than her, flimsier. Like someone had butchered the legs halfway through the craft and forgot the creature needed them to stand. An afterthought of a monster. For some reason, Jackie kept her head down. Ears burning. She lifted her eyes and saw the cube of her stomach on the creature's, heaving like some newborn baby. But it had no true face, no mouth. So who was speaking? The creature moaned, almost friendly, and walked away from her, towards the glass. Glass. A window. On the other side, open eyes and mouths. Horrified expressions.

"Jackie! What the hell? What is this? Oh god—"

The thing looked back at her, ashamed. It cried, if you could say such a sound was crying. It stared at her with her labia on its nose and her mismatched stomach and her blood and her left ear and wailed. She wanted to hit it, hard. She wanted to kill it. Grabbed the knife through her jacket. And something stopped her. It was hers after all. *Her* creation. Dread overcame her, first in sweat, then a spell of nausea. Against her will, she hurled in front of the wall. Cornmeal-colored chunks slid down the once pristine window. Her family, her ex, his wife, her friends, her dance teacher.

They could see it. They could always see it.

Then the monster approached her and plucked her blade from her jacket. Her mind raced, a chorus of angry priests. *Oh, you thought you could hide things away, pretend they never happened? You thought, you thought? Didn't anyone tell you? Darkness hides those things that require hiding, but they never disappear. Darkness is light in waiting.*

"What are you doing?" She pleaded.

But the creature moved in a way that soothed her. Kind, understanding, merciful. Two hands, all wrong and rodent-like, held the blade against her lips. Sliced her mouth right off. Jackie looked out at the window, crying. Her hands smeared two greasy prints on the window. She looked out—the dark stain of regret where her mouth should be. The people on the other side watched in terror.

"Grotesque! Disgusting!" They couldn't look away.

And the creature? Stood there and plastered the limp mouth where its face should be. Started talking back to her, with her voice.

Everyone can see it. Everyone can see you.

Everyone can see it. Everyone can see you.

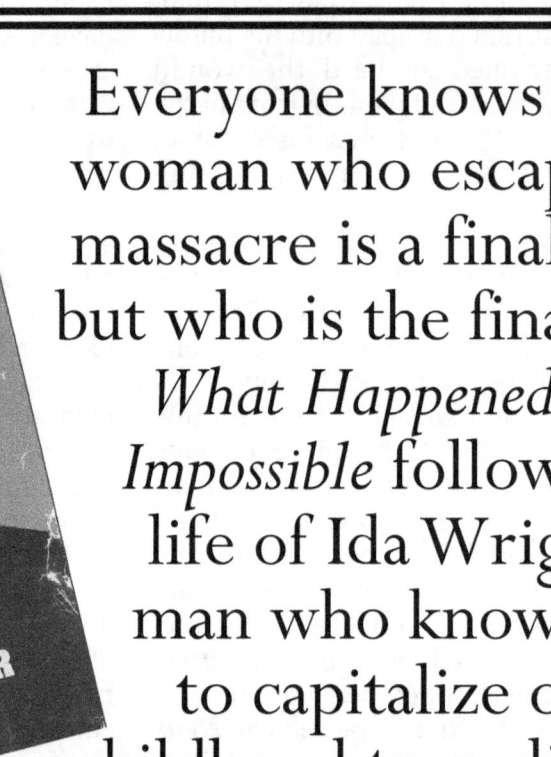

One brooding summer, Nadine Boone pricks herself on a poisonous manchineel tree in the Florida backcountry. Upon self-orgasm, Nadine conjures a witch that she calls Saint Grit. Pitched as Gummo meets The Craft, Saint Grit grows inside of Nadine over three decades, wreaking repulsive havoc on a suspicious cast of characters in a small town known as Sugar Bends.

COMING OCTOBER 2023

Leo Bates knows what's behind every corner in her hometown of Eston, Maine, where she's lived her whole life. Some bad memories and grief for her late parents, sure, but nothing dangerous. Nothing unexplainable.

All of that changes when her girlfriend Tate goes missing, and the lead detective on the case blames Leo for the disappearance. Haunted by self-doubt, Leo can only watch as the town she thought she knew deteriorates around her. She is forced to confront the painful truth about her parents, this town, and her relationship if she is to survive the following onslaught of conspiracies, cryptic monstrosities, and whatever is hiding in the woods where Tate was last seen.

The familiar becomes strange the longer you look at it. Leo navigates a broken sense of reality, shattered memories, and a distrust of herself in order to find Tate and restore balance to Eston—if such a thing ever existed to begin with.

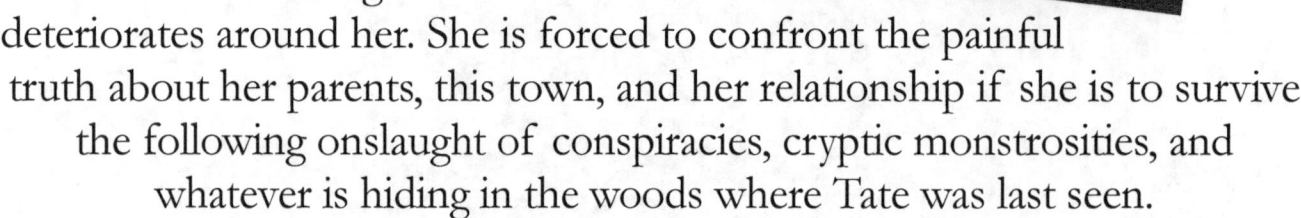

WWW.GHOULISHBOOKS.COM

THE KOJI SHOW

Angela Liu

WHEN MAMI SHOWS me the ad, I'm skeptical: $5,000 for a ninety-minute stint, twice a week, guaranteed for the next fifty-two weeks. My math's never been so good, but I got Mami punching the numbers into her fancy school calculator, and we're looking at $260,000 over the next year. That's enough to pay back the debt *and* still go on that father-daughter vacation to Japan so we can see the famed giant robot.

"All you gotta do is play the world's biggest loser ghost in some dude's creepy self-written play," Mami says, thumb-typing her latest blog entry into her phone. "You've probably done worse."

I'm offended she doesn't even try to look like she's kidding when she says that. But a father takes what he can.

***

The dude's name is John Babouzakuro. I got the feeling it's a fake name, but hey we all got our reasons. He's the one with the fat checkbook, so I'll call him Elvis Presley if he wants.

I ain't Julliard-trained, but I got my pride. I've been acting since college. I blame it on Ms. Farrow, the 80-year-old sponge-faced prof from my Acting 1.0 elective at NYU during freshman year. The mummy's got a way with words, all "Koji, you've got a special talent," and "Koji, you could move people to tears with just your eyes," and "Koji, I think you should come to my private classes in Chelsea. The first month is free."

Once I start something, I ain't a quitter. So twenty years later, here I am. On a bus to some dude's house in Queens for an audition, trying to eat my quarter pounder while a wild-eyed baby stares up at me from his stroller like he can see the Holy Spirit itself hovering above my head. Outside the window, it's all *Sound of Music* sun and blue sky, except instead of Julie Andrews belting out Do-Re-Mis, there's a guy blaring some song about big butts on his portable speaker.

John Babouzakuro is watering plants outside his house when I arrive.

"You're early," he says without looking up.

"Sorry, should I come back?"

He shakes his head, sniffing some roses before motioning for me to follow him into the house.

"Have you ever played a ghost before?" he asks as we walk down the dimly-lit hall. It smells like the Chinese medicine/bootleg DVD shop near Mami's favorite popcorn chicken place on Roosevelt Ave.

"My last role was this ghost who was haunting Christopher Columbus," I answer, dodging a mountain of cardboard boxes, trying to keep up. The guy's a fast walker. "It was a modern take with a couple of rap songs, and Christopher Columbus was actually the head of this huge evil online shopping site. We did it at some community center near Delancey and there was even a big dance number at the end, so we all learned a bit of breakdancing."

Koji Yamadera and Tammy Fraser were great as the two loan shark ghosts who come to Columbus during a cocaine-fueled dream. That's what the *Washington Village Times* wrote in their review. I ain't gonna brag, but Mom kept a closet empty as a spare room for dead visitors, so I think I've been method acting this ghost thing for a couple of decades.

In the living room, a black and white printout of my Twitter profile photo sits in a wooden frame like a funeral altar, a couple of incense sticks burning in front of it. Monk chanting throbs out of a laptop on the couch, playing from a YouTube clip.

"This role will be a bit different," John says, fanning the snaking incense smoke toward his nostrils.

"So, uh, about the audition . . . " I say, trying to keep my cool.

He holds up a hand, eyes closed, nostrils still flaring. "No need. You've received a glowing recommendation. The role is yours. I hope you're up for the challenge."

"Absolutely, sir. You're not an artist if you're not being challenged," I say, paraphrasing one of Ms. Farrow's old speeches. May the old bat rest in peace.

***

There's a total of four of us, including John. Mary plays the unhappy wife (and an unhappier accountant in real life). Rui, who's got godly looks and a brain like a soggy zucchini, plays the evil but impressionable lover. And finally, me, the unattractive but hardworking husband who ends up murdered by the zucchini, er, attractive lover and spends more than half the play wearing a tasseled burlap bag, haunting the scheming couple like a personified fungal infection. John Babouzakuro throws on a Zara meets Grim Reaper black turtleneck get-up and narrates from the stage wings (and when there aren't any, he sits in the audience and narrates, which always gets a couple of 'ohhh, cool, he's part of the play! so interactive!').

Mami came to our first show at the Flushing Community Center with her mom and her mom's new fancy boyfriend with the Apple Watch, good teeth and posture like he's a runner, and not a from-the-debtors kind. Good for them, I guess. Mami gave a thumbs up review on her blog. I bought her a new phone with my first paycheck, so now she's Koji the Ghost's #1 fan.

We do shows throughout Queens and Brooklyn, one on Friday night, the other's a Sunday matinee. Tilly, the ghoulish old lady who runs the Babouzakuro office/home/rehearsal prison and never speaks in anything more than displeased grunts, stays in the car during our ninety-minute performance, ready to move if the cops come. Friday nights bring in mostly artsy college kids and younger couples, all hand-holding and giggly like happy dolphins. The Sunday matinees are the worst, filled with miserable tourists who bought the wrong tickets online (with a show name like *The Phantom*, who can blame them?) and old people tipsy from brunch who have magically forgotten how loud their voices are.

We've gotten a few one-starred reviews from local newspapers, which doesn't upset John. He says it's only a matter of time. Mary and I don't have a clue about what he means, but Rui's neck-deep in conspiracy theories, so he thinks John's talking about the arrival of the wormholes, that we're all going to have to leave this world to save another sometime soon.

"Our bodies will have to *ascend*," he says, wolfing down a vegan protein bar. "We won't have a choice."

"Our bodies would likely be torn to bits if forced through a wormhole," Mary sighs, memo-ing her lunch receipt into her phone.

The $5000's in my bank account every Tuesday morning, so I got no complaints.

***

Sometimes I wake up with weird patches on my arms and legs, like bruises that I don't remember getting. They don't hurt and by the next day, they're usually gone.

"Hey, it's like free make-up!" Rui laughed when I showed them to him before a show. "You should wear shorts and a t-shirt to show them off! It's summer after all!"

"You really don't have any recollection of where they came from?" Mary chimed in like a nervous mom, her crocheting needles clicking, a rainbow-colored mini polo shirt the size of a ghost baby in her lap. "I heard there's some disease where you might hurt yourself without even realizing, like you take on a whole other personality. My dad's been spending too much time on Web MD, and he sends me links of the diseases he thinks he might have. Dissociative Disorder or something like that."

"Dissocia-what?" Sounded like an 80s band. "Nah, this ain't some disease. Doesn't even hurt."

Mary made a disapproving sound at the back of her throat like Mami's mom used to.

"Costumes on!" John clapped from the stage, and that was the end of that.

***

Mami and I haven't had a father-daughter trip since she was still small enough to fall asleep during the fights her mom and I had, so I want to plan a good one. All fancy, Instagrammable meals, like that train that brings around your sushi or the octopus that dances on top of your rice before you eat it. A nice hotel where they change your sheets every night and everyone smells like pine trees. Heck, Mami's only really started talking to me since I got this job, so this is my chance to make things right between us.

"Hey, come get a drink with me," John calls when I'm looking up plane tickets to Tokyo.

John Babouzakuro doesn't usually drink, so I'm intrigued.

We meet at a divey bar near his house. Red spotlights, $3 whiskey shots, watered down beer on tap, and a bunch of plaid-shirted guys gathered around the bar talking about NFTs and how to smoke a watermelon. There's a rusty sign behind the counter that reads 'Hell Is Here,' which I like.

"I got you a new costume idea for the last show," John says, passing me a drink, froth dribbling over the sides of the glass.

"I like the swamp monster-look I got going now," I say, gulping down half the glass so it's easier to hold. The beer's got a dishwater meets rusted nails kinda mouthfeel.

John looks at his hands. They're big and scarred from god knows what kind of work he did before he decided to write his own play. The bar's red lights make him look bloodied.

"You've been trying your best. You all have. But I dunno, it just doesn't feel right. Like something's missing," he says.

Now I feel bad. I know what he means. Mary's got bad nerves (I've caught her yelling at herself in the mirror a few times when she thinks no one's around). Rui gets batshit crazy sometimes (talking about aliens and microchipped pillows spying on his dreams when he hasn't gotten enough sleep). Even Tilly, the old hag, is researching tombstones

during her lunch break. We ain't exactly a Class A team of Oscar-hopefuls. Still, we do our best. We ain't bad people.

"Phantom forever!" I shout, not knowing what I mean, but it sounds right. A couple of the plaid-shirted guys glance over like they're praying a fight breaks out so they can punch someone tonight. Too bad, fellas. "We're the best show in Queens. And we're gonna be the best show in NYC! Just let me know what you want me to do, and I'll do it."

"I think the costume will help you up your acting game," John says. "I'll have someone bring it over to your apartment tomorrow morning. Oh, it'd also be great if you didn't wash your hair until the next show."

"My hair's gonna feel like fire ants're crawling—"

"Just this once," John says, handing me an envelope. He gestures for me to open it. Inside there are so many $100 bills that I'm afraid to count.

"What's this for?"

"An advance," he says over the roar of a neighboring table doing another round of whiskey shots.

***

The new costume smells like strawberries and marijuana. In that way, it's kinda nostalgic. It smells like my old man's house. His girlfriend liked strawberry-flavored lip gloss. She was also twenty-five years younger than him and my mom's yoga teacher, but hey, we can't help the people we wanna bang.

But back to the outfit. I'm not sure you could call it that since it's mainly a straitjacket with a special release on the inside so I can get out of it myself if I need to.

My hair looks as nasty as if feels, like a tattered cafeteria rag used to wipe up a sick kid's vomit.

"You look good! The straitjacket's got a super *vibe*," Rui says when I'm done changing. He looks like a movie star in his new suit and slicked back hair, all he needs to do is keep his mouth shut and he'd be swimming in job offers.

"The straitjacket does add some uniqueness. You went from being just a ghost to being a mentally ill ghost that may or may not have insurance to cover the hospital stay and prescribed medications it needs," Mary says, staring bleakly at the buckles on the jacket. She doesn't really talk about her family, but we can tell from the screaming phone calls filtering out from the lady's room (John thinks the paper-thin walls at the office build community) that stuff's not so hot at Chez Mary these days. Something about Stage 4 or 3 or 0, I dunno, someone's dying. Probably. None of us have the guts to ask.

John tells me the other two will get new costumes soon, too. We'll be a bonafide theater troupe, complete with a costume change.

There's a fat storm cloud the size of Brooklyn overhead waiting to let loose. Today we're doing our Sunday matinee in the parking lot outside Citi Field.

The crowd's pretty bare bones. Just a few drunks who thought Mary looked hot and a couple of tourists that ain't willing to let the shit weather get in their way to an authentic "New York" experience.

John says this'll be a good trial run. Test drive the new costume with a small group so we can make any necessary adjustments. He says we're going be huge. That we're going to bring this show to Broadway, Lincoln Center, Carnegie Hall, the Apollo Theater—he talks about these places the way my mom used to whisper the name of holy saints during lottery number drawing days.

The parking lot stage is lined with metal rods.

Mary seems antsy, something about not having insurance and fire hazards, but Rui thinks the stage looks *Game of Thrones*-ish.

John rounds us up like a high school hockey coach.

"You've all done a great job," he says, passing us each a gold-lined metal pin with the 'Phantom' logo on it to put on our costumes. Rui looks genuinely moved. "Life's tough, but it's been a good year. We've become a real team. I think we're gonna finish off our last performance of the season with a bang."

"Yeah! We're gonna blow them away!" Mary says, trying to be more enthusiastic like her supervisor at the accounting firm recommended during her job evaluation.

"I can't believe it's already been a year," Rui says, teary-eyed, his slicked hair already sticking up like a dollar store duster. "I'm gonna miss you guys."

"Hey, this is just a beginning!" I say, shoulder-bumping him since my arms are tied up in the straitjacket.

The three of us do something like an awkward battle cry, the sound of donkeys getting slaughtered, and I think John smiles for the first time.

***

I message Mami with a photo of the three of us, the Citi Field stadium behind us, Rui waving the prop ax he uses to murder me in the play.

She doesn't respond for a while, and I start worrying about that new male friend she said she's been "studying" with a lot lately. Ain't nothing a teenage boy wants to study more than the slick lines on a teenage girl's body.

"Good luck 🌝," she finally types back. "Don't let us down!"

Us? "Any funny business with the boyfriend, and I'm gonna come haunt you two 👻," I type back, but she doesn't respond.

***

The rain comes barreling down, drenching us. Mini lakes cover the parking lot. Half an hour in, even the hecklers flee. John waves to us from the audience in a canary yellow rain poncho.

Keep going, he mouths.

Mary shouts something back, but I can barely hear a thing over the rain.

The straitjacket's too tight and there's rainwater in my mouth and eyes. I tell myself it's nothing compared to the time Ms. Farrow had me pull on a pair of dancer tights and play one of Romeo's henchmen for her annual holiday party show. We danced and served little wiener and cheese snacks to a mash-up of Hakuna Matata and DMX, until one of the guests smashed an empty champagne bottle over my head. I saw lightning then, like the guests were exploding around me, all melting eye sockets and skin—the Doc later said that was just the concussion. Had to get six stitches. The guest, all fancy suit and superhero jaw, claimed he thought the bottle was just a prop, but cackled about it with his friends in the bathroom afterwards. Shit happens, what can you do? Being a nobody's tough.

I've come a long way since then. The scars don't even really hurt anymore.

Lightning streaks across the purple sky in

consecutive flashes, the whole world a strobing nightclub. The flashes get brighter, the space between them shorter.

Then my eyes white-out—the light reaches me before the heat, before the earth-shattering sound. A 300-million-volt lightning bolt strikes one of the standing metal rods and sends our entire wet stage ablaze.

I can't hear or see a thing. But I smell something. The charred, throat-scratching smell of something burning.

It's me. I'm burning. The rain boils against my skin. I think I'm dying. But still alive. Alive but dying. I can't think straight, everything hurts, hurts, hurts, fuck it hurts. What about Rui and Mary? The stench of burnt flesh is everywhere.

I don't wanna die. I don't wanna die. Idontwannadie.

We're gonna be huge. Please, please, please.

***

"How do you feel?" John asks, hovering over me. The rain's just a foggy mist now. My ears are still ringing.

"Kinda nauseous," I croak, everything aches but by some miracle, I'm alive.

"Good. That means your insides are still intact. I'm glad the costume worked."

"The what?" My mouth tastes like copper coins.

"There's no point in playing a ghost unless you can play the best ghost, yes?"

"I guess so—" I swallow and my ears pop painfully. "But what the hell happened to everyone?"

"I've decided to renew the show for another year."

"Great," I say, trying to sit, but my stomach feels steamrolled. "Where's Rui and Sergeant Mary?" I cough out a laugh. Maybe we can all go out to that dive bar in celebration, squeeze out a round of free drinks from Mr. Babouzakuro.

"Mary and Rui didn't survive the challenge, unfortunately, but I've already got two new actors to take their place. No big deal."

"What?" I swallow again. My throat feels like sandpaper. "I mean I'm fine, but I kinda liked them."

"Don't worry, you won't even remember them by the end of the day."

"What do you mean?"

"Tilly deals with the administrative side, contract renewals, severances, funerals, memory clean-ups and all that, so you would have to ask her for the details."

"I don't understand." My brain doesn't want to be a part of this conversation. "I wanna go home and take a shower."

"I'm afraid you won't be going home for a while. Don't worry, the money will continue to be deposited in your account. Mami's been given all the information."

"Mami? She's still in high school." Now I'm annoyed. How does he even know her name? "You got any idea what a kid's gonna do with access to that kind of money? Her mom will fucking kill me."

"Mr. Koji," he says. I realize it's the first time he's ever said my name. "Your daughter seems quite competent with her own finances. She also truly believes in your potential. She told me that when she signed you up for our experiment."

"Experiment?"

I can hear my own breathing, like the wheezing of a car engine in the winter.

"We've tentatively named it *The Koji Show*. We're testing how deeply a person can dip a foot into the grave before it finally takes them. The technology is there, but some say it's dangerous and unethical blahblahblah," he answers, puppeting a Venus flytrap with his hands. "We've booked venues throughout the States, a traveling experiment sold as an unforgettable show. We'll show them all the ways you can die without dying. A real ghost, the best. Your show will be huge, and you'll be the star. Isn't that what you've always wanted?" He dusts something off my shoulders. Maybe a wet leaf. Maybe singed flesh. I push aside the image of Rui and Mary in their costumes like flicking off a bad television show or closing a spam browser. Ms. Farrow called it Motivated Forgetting. *It takes a special talent to forget who you are,* the old hag said, *to really become something else entirely.*

"I'll be the best ghost," I say, pride welling in my paper-thin chest. I raise a fist toward the sky, another silent flash of lightning answering. My hand is a bubbly mess of brown-black spots and fleshy sores. But hey, free make-up, yeah? "Let's give 'em a show."

"I like that energy," John says, the floodlights of the stadium beaming on behind him. A car pulls up next to us. "Keep it going. Forever."

When Tilly comes out, her face doesn't look right, Mr. John neither, like funhouse mirror people. The stadium lights behind the fog sputters like faulty angel halos. I can't feel my fingers or feet, but don't sweat the details, yeah? I'm the greatest actor, and I ain't a quitter.

Would really you want

your book to look

like this?

No, of course not!

You've worked hard to complete your masterpiece.

Make it look as professional as you are.

www.TheAuthorsAlley.com

HEARTBEAT

Chloe Harper Gold

IT HAD A heartbeat.

The image on the screen was a grainy black and white, but there it was. An almost imperceptible flicker that they told me was proof of life. The doctor congratulated me with a wide smile that showed too many teeth. He called me *Mom* and scheduled three follow-up appointments, choosing the dates and times himself without asking for my input. It didn't matter; I wouldn't be going to any of them. He wrote down recommendations for vitamins and supplements and exercises and books. Jotted down things to avoid, like soft cheeses and hot baths and trampolines. He handed me the paper. I spit my gum into it.

The thing inside me wouldn't be getting any special vitamins. I wasn't going to alter my yoga routine to accommodate it. It wouldn't be staying long. One way or another, I was going to get it out.

I started smoking more, going from three daily cigarettes to nine, and switched from my usual organic brand that boasted 100% GREEN. 100% CLEAN on the pack to one that didn't make sustainability claims and didn't have filter tips. I limited myself to 500 calories a day and supplemented with caffeine pills. Drank bourbon straight from the bottle. Treated myself to lines of blow and tabs of acid and ecstasy pills in the shape of rainbows. I resurrected my college years habit of starting each morning with a tequila shot and a bong hit.

I kept it up for four months and nevertheless, the little shit persisted. I upped the ante. I brewed mugs of pennyroyal tea and drank them while I soaked in tubs filled with scalding hot water. Stood in front of the microwave for ten minutes at a time. Micro-dosed arsenic and foxglove. Huffed insecticide. Ignored call after call from the doctor. Steadied my pulse by reminding myself that I had written a fake address on my intake form.

I resented it for taking so much of my time and energy. I threw myself into my work, taking on new jobs and new clients. I tried to convince myself that this reignited enthusiasm for web design came from a desire for designer clothes and vintage handbags. But really, it was because whenever my thoughts weren't occupied with coding they went straight to the parasite. I was caught in a never-ending loop of *What should I do differently? Why isn't anything working? What if it just won't give up?*

Anger brewed within me, claiming as much of my body as the growing thing did. I hoped that it felt my anger. I hoped that it felt every poison I swallowed and smoked. I wanted to kill it. But even more, I wanted to hurt it. I wanted it to be in excruciating pain and I wanted to be the direct cause of it. I wanted it to be in such agony that it ripped itself apart. I imagined my anger and my hatred filling up my womb and suffocating it.

My days were awful. But late nights were the worst. Late nights were when anger rested and anxiety took over. My mind drifted to old novels that referenced homes for unwed mothers. To movies that joked about shotgun weddings. To my grandmother's chilling stories about back-alley botch jobs. For the first time, I was glad that my grandmother was dead; if she had known I was in this mess it would have killed her.

A particularly bad night brought on a panic attack when I realized that if I couldn't kill this thing in utero, I would have to give birth to it and kill it then. It would be for the best. It would undoubtedly be too damaged to live very long anyway. FUBAR, as one might put it. I imagined bearing down, reaching between my legs, and pulling out a limp, almost empty husk of skin containing only half-formed bones, disintegrating organs, and a beating heart. Killing it would be the kindest thing to do. I would do it quickly, before it could even draw a breath. *If* it could even draw a breath.

I would have to kill it before I could do something stupid. Like hold it. Like look at its face, if it even had a face.

The thought of killing it wasn't the cause of the panic attack. The fear that I wouldn't be able to do it was.

I was determined to get this thing out of me by any means necessary. My friends packed overnight bags and stayed with me to make sure I didn't accidentally kill myself in the process. Maya suggested acupuncture. Justine looked up bus routes and train schedules and plane tickets using a tool that would render the search untraceable. Lacey offered up a knitting needle, a wire hanger, and a gentle push down the stairs.

"I asked my cousin in Vancouver if she could send some pills here," Justine said. "She said she'll try."

"Maybe you could try cohosh," Maya said. "I think I remember reading about it in a zine."

"Blue cohosh or black?" I asked. Maya bit her lip as she mulled it over.

"I guess you could try both?"

I grew more and more nauseous by the day. I imagined my teeth eroding little by little, from enamel to root, until they crumbled to bits in my mouth and fell down my throat like a rockslide. My feet and ankles became swollen and splotchy red. Blue-black varicose veins snaked up my calves. My ribs creaked and strained under the new heaviness of my breasts. My stomach, once flat with protruding hip bones, transformed before my eyes to distended ruin.

"You don't look *that* bad," Lacey said. "Hey, at least your skin isn't breaking out like my sister's did!"

I could feel the thing moving around inside of me, writhing and squirming like a tapeworm. It had taken me hostage, destroying my body and stealing everything vital within it. I had vivid dreams of psychedelic monsters. Of trippy leeches and glitching hellhounds that sparkled with static. I had recurring nightmares of getting caught in spiderwebs made of bubblegum pink barbed wire.

Seven months after I saw the heartbeat, the thing that had been growing inside of me finally made its exit.

The doctor, distressed and frantic that I hadn't been returning his calls or showing up to appointments, arrived at my doorstep red-faced and panting. He forced his way past Justine to get inside, intent on assisting me in the miracle of bringing forth new life into the world. He had been trying to track me down for months, he explained through his wheezing. He said he understood that it was trendy these days to carry a pregnancy naturally, honoring our foremothers and all that, but, really, consulting with an expert (like him, for example) was in everyone's best interest. And, he added, he had my best interests at heart; mine and the little bundle of joy's.

I was in agony, on all fours sweating and moaning and gasping while Lacey dabbed at my forehead with a cool washcloth. My insides were burning and twisting. I thought for sure that the latest dose of poison was finally working. Maya stood by, stock still and tense. A cigarette in one hand and the phone in the other, getting ready to call for either an ambulance or my mother.

As the doctor stepped closer, the pain traveled downward, morphing into an unbearable and ever-increasing pressure. I tried to stand. I had an urge to squat that was too overwhelming and primordial to resist. Lacey, Justine, and Maya surrounded me in an instant, holding me up, holding my hands, baring their teeth at the doctor. They threatened him with poison, with knitting needles, with a shove down the concrete basement stairs. There was no doubt in my mind that they would follow through if it came to that. I would do the same for them. My closest friends. My protectors. My co-conspirators. *This is the end*, I thought. *This is the end the end the end.*

And then suddenly the pain gave way to the sensation of something gelatinous slipping out of my body and falling to the floor between my knees with a *splat*. The force of the expulsion slid it a few inches across the hardwood. My knees buckled. I would have fallen to the floor had it not been for my friends' iron grips on my arms and waist. I steadied my breath. I laughed in relief.

And then I saw what had slithered out of me.

It was a tiny little thing, so covered in slime it looked almost shapeless. We all watched in silence as it began to unfold itself in fluid and unnervingly precise movements. It had four spidery limbs and an oblong skull. A long, rail-thin torso and a twitching tail, all held together with translucent, holographic skin. It turned to me and blinked the blood out of neon green eyes. Opened and closed its mouth a few times, showing off rows of pointy teeth with serrated edges. Flexed and clenched its hands. Stretched its spine like a cat.

And then lunged at the doctor and bit out chunks of his throat.

Maya and Justine screamed. Lacey and I stared in awe at the thing that I had created, inadvertently and unwillingly. The creature—my baby, the fruit of my womb—looked at the four of us and let out a croaky, gleeful shriek.

Through its skin, we saw its heart beat.

THE WEREWOLF'S GUIDE TO NEW YORK CRIMINAL LAW

Nicholas A. Battaglia

IT IS WELL-ESTABLISHED that ignorance of the law is not a defense—whether you are human or werewolf. Although most people may never need a criminal defense lawyer, the same is not true for lycanthropes. The inherent and customary lives of werewolves naturally increase the risk that, at some point in his or her life, a werewolf will run afoul with the criminal law in New York. These increased risks include everything from the obvious assault charges, to innocent pitfalls involving bestiality or even just burning a mongrel's trash before bed. The unfortunate truth for a werewolf is that, even for a minor charge that may carry with it a minimal term of incarceration, if that incarceration occurs during an unfortunate time in the moon cycle, it is likely that a werewolf will pick up other—unavoidable—charges while incarcerated that may result in a longer term of incarceration. That means every criminal charge should be avoided at all costs for a werewolf. We hope this guide can help you and your family navigate the complex matrix of the criminal laws in New York, allowing you to better manage these risks to avoid unnecessary interaction with law enforcement which often go poorly for werewolves.

We'll start with a brief but important primer on New York law. The statutory law, or the body of law made through the formal rule-making process by the Legislature, is the fundamental source of the criminal laws in New York. These criminal laws are recorded in what is known as the Penal Law, the body of code which sets forth specific criminal offenses, their defenses, and the penalties for violating same. The statutory laws are then interpreted by the courts through judicial decision-making, where court rulings and written decisions become part of the common law. Other sources of law which may embody criminal offenses that are relevant to werewolves include regulatory rules (promulgated by agencies) and municipal law (passed by villages, towns, cities, and counties). Therefore, our guide of New York criminal law will consider and apply the statutory law as interpreted by courts.

I. Assault and Menacing

Assault is the first substantive area of law applicable to werewolves. It is governed by article 120 of the Penal Law, and encompasses acts causing a victim physical injury in an intentional, reckless, or criminally negligent manner. There are multiple degrees of assault and variations of assault that are applied in certain situations, such as gang assault. The degree of which a werewolf may be charged with assault depends on several factors, including the severity of the injury, whether a weapon was used, and the mental culpability (*mens rea*) of a Lycan in committing the offense.

All assaults require some level of physical injury, which is defined as "impairment of physical condition or substantial pain" (NY Penal Law § 10.00 [9]). Notably, this does not include bruises (*see People v Boney*, 119 AD3d 701 [2d Dept 2014]) or superficial cuts and punctures (*see People v Ferrer*, 84 AD3d 1396 [2d Dept 2011]). Nor will petty slaps, shoves, kicks, or similar conduct be considered sufficient enough to cause "substantial pain" (see Matter of Philip A., 49 NY2d 198 [1980]). Whereas a torn tendon or superficial injury restricting movement of a limb may constitute a physical injury (see People v Williams, 46 AD3d 1115 [3d Dept 2007]). Thus, it is prudent that any werewolf bite or scratch be skin-deep, not penetrating to tissue below and not causing permanent scarring—especially to the face. Open palm slaps, channeling your Herculean strength but not your hardened nails, can be used to strike or shove another in a manner to also not satisfy the definition of a physical injury. Conscious effort should be used to temporarily stun or disable another, but not cause lasting injury that is more than a superficial wound.

This leads to another important part of an assault charge, a deadly weapon or dangerous instrument. Under New York law, a deadly weapon typically includes a firearm, type of fixed blade, or club (see NY Penal Law § 10.00 [12]). But where a werewolf could earn an elevated charge is with a "dangerous instrument," which is defined as "any instrument, article or substance . . . which, under the circumstances in which it is used, attempted to be used or threatened to be used, is readily capable of causing death or other serious physical injury" (NY Penal Law § 10.00 [13]). A dangerous instrument is not a hand (see People v Petrosino, 299 AD2d 851 [4th Dept 2002]) or even natural teeth (see People v Owusu, 93 NY2d 398 [1999]). Although a court has yet to interpret whether a werewolf's teeth may constitute a dangerous instrument, currently the precedent is that natural teeth are not a separate instrument. Thus, as noted above, it would be prudent for a werewolf to limit the use of teeth to inflict any type of injury on another.

It would further be best practice to not use one's Lycan fingernails, as—although fingernails may not constitute a dangerous instrument—a werewolf's fingernails are more akin to claws, which may cause lacerations that may suggest a bladed weapon was used and well-hidden (see People v Pagan, 163 AD2d 681 [3d Dept 1990]). This would require a werewolf to rebut that presumption or prove that such fingernails (claws) were a natural extension of his or her body, a difficult inquiry to satisfy in a court of law. Moreover, it should be noted that not all fingernail-caused injuries will avoid an assault charge, as scraping out someone's eye out with just fingernails may still, hypothetically, result in an assault charge (see, i.e., U.S. v Sturgis, 48 F3d 784 [1995]). It is further important to recognize that a dangerous instrument can extend beyond a werewolf's body or what he or she may be carrying. For instance, if a werewolf uses an open palm strike to knock down another, it would be best not to jump, pounce, kick, punch, or otherwise strike that individual against that ground, as a sidewalk, curb, or parking lot could constitute a dangerous instrument (see People v Melville, 298 AD2d 601 [2d Dept 2002]).

As a final note, article 120 of the Penal Law also contains the criminal offense known as menacing. This is any conduct that places another in fear of physical injury or death. Arguably, a werewolf's physical attributes could constitute menacing per se. That's unfair, as it is a natural presentation of one's Lycan attributes, but it is one that could be elevated by engaging in snarling, growling, howling, or flashing of claws, teeth, or flexing those varnished muscles. Since menacing does not require any injury, a werewolf should not engage in any conduct that may be interpreted as threatening. That may even include lunging or walking in the direction of another while in any shapeshifted form. It further goes without saying that even threatening to rip apart, tear, bite, or otherwise harm another person—even if you don't do it—can still constitute menacing (see Matter of Willie W., 32 AD3d 479 [2d Dept 2006]).

II. Bestiality and Sexual Offenses

An unfortunate area of criminal exposure for any shapeshifter is bestiality, technically a form of sexual misconduct in New York. Section 130.20 of the New York Penal Law governs sexual misconduct, and provides that a person (or werewolf) is guilty of this offense when under sub(3) "[h]e or she engaged in sexual conduct with an animal or a dead human body." Where shapeshifters such as werewolves run afoul with this is when, during sexual relations, one werewolf remains in a human, un-shapeshifted form, but a partner has transformed and remains in wolf-form. Since the law's definition of a person or human does not encompass a werewolf, technically that would mean a werewolf would constitute an animal. Accordingly, intercourse between two consenting individuals—one in human form and one in werewolf form—would constitute sexual misconduct.

As such, the best practice would be for all partners engaged in relations to be in the same form. This may be difficult in the feral heat of the moment, especially under a starry full moon background, but it would be prudent to avoid this offense as it is a class A misdemeanor which is punishable up to one year in prison. It is axiomatic that, given the unavoidable moon cycle, a werewolf won't likely serve a one-year sentence without harming another inmate or correction officer and earning new charges.

III. Trash Burning

Although the best practice is to burn one's trash before bed, there are statutory, regulatory, and municipal perils for werewolves doing this. Under the New York Penal Law, section 240.20 which governs "disorderly conduct" may apply in certain urban or suburban areas. Specifically, subsection (7) provides that a person (or werewolf) is "guilty of disorderly conduct when, with intent to cause public inconvenience, annoyance or alarm, or recklessly creating a risk thereof, "[h]e creates a hazardous of physically offense condition by any act which serves no legitimate purpose." Even though burning trash has quite important Lycanthropic purposes, it has no legitimate purpose for humans. This section has further been interpreted that spreading trash or noxious substances (including smoke), can be sufficient to charge an individual (or werewolf) with disorderly conduct (see People v Cooke, 152 Misc.2d 311 [1991]). It so follows that dumping trash in a burn pile or burn hole and then igniting it would likely satisfy the elements of disorderly conduct, resulting in criminal charges.

But more troubling are the prohibitions imposed by the New York State Department of Environment Conversation (DEC). The regulations promulgated by this administrative agency prohibit any person from burning or allowing to be burned "any materials in an open fire" (6 NYCRR § 215.2). This has been interpreted to include trash, which is not an enumerated and permissible material to burn under the list of such exceptions (see 6 NYCRR § 215.3). Further, the DEC imposes a complete burn ban from March 16 through May 14 each year, which could include permissible fires under section 215.3. Many municipalities also echo these prohibitions, sometimes extending them before the March date or after the May date, or even imposing local burn restrictions outside of these times when weather conditions warrant such a prohibition. Any werewolves burning anything—trash or not—during these prohibitions could face criminal charges or fines.

This presents a difficult challenge for werewolves and shapeshifters, particularly in urban and suburban settings. Certain materials, such as aluminum and metals, can burn obnoxiously and leave significant-enough traces that the prying eyes of a police officer or detective may find sufficient to bring charges. Other materials, such as styrofoam or treated wood, will create significant plumes and odiferous conditions that even a non-Lycan human would be able to smell from that proverbial mile away. Although a solution may appear to keep such burning inside the home or masked by a wood fire, one would be keen to ensure all ventilation systems are sufficient to push any noxious fumes up and out of the home. Notwithstanding, it is still noted that this solution is still not a legal one. Best practice would therefore be to keep trash and straps disposed in a locked box or can, that is inaccessible to even the most intrepid of shapeshifters. It would then be important that werewolves are studious in disposing of trash on the applicable trash pickup days, or skipping these pickup days entirely when they align with the moon's cycle. This would be the only legal way of handling a mongrel's trash.

IV. A Note on Homicide

Where a werewolf's actions result in the death of a human, the perilous web of New York homicide laws create a sticky and often inescapable trap. This is for the inherent reason that most juries—who are not of *your* Lycan peers—would be hard-pressed to find that a werewolf did not act with the necessary mental state to cause the death of another. Said differently, most triers of fact will find that a werewolf is an inherently dangerous and deadly humanoid that is very capable of murder, already pre-disposed with a depraved indifference. This is, of course, not a fair assessment because it creates a legal presumption where none exists. But this is an unfortunate stereotype that is ingrained in a layperson's mind.

This does not mean that there is no applicable defense in certain cases. For instance, even though a werewolf's intimidating shapeshifted-form may easily sustain charges for menacing, that is not true if such intimidation causes the victim to die from a heart attack instead (*see People v Davis*, 126 AD3d 1516 [4th Dept 2015]). Moreover, where a victim is armed with a firearm (even if not loaded with silver-plated ammunition), the defense of justification may be applicable. This defense allows a person (or werewolf) to defend himself or herself from an imminent threat of seriously bodily harm or death. A victim brandishing a firearm, even at a werewolf, would likely constitute a sufficient-enough threat to permit a werewolf to use deadly force to protect himself or herself. This is, however, hypothetical in application, as other factors as to who created the threat first (i.e., the werewolf or the victim's firearm), may present a question of fact for a trier of fact. This, again, leads to the presumption that most laypeople may have as a juror that werewolves are indeed inherently dangerous. Accordingly, although the very feral nature of werewolves may lead to homicide, it is best to remove oneself from situations conducive to friction where someone could, in fact, be killed.

V. Conclusion

Werewolves in New York need to take note of all of the applicable laws to protect themselves and their families. Even minor offenses with seemingly short sentences of incarceration can, if at an unfortunate time during the moon cycle, lead to worse offenses that lead to greater terms of incarceration. It should further be recognized that, although New York does not engage in capital punishment, that applies to humans. It is unclear how a werewolf will be treated, as New York law does permit dangerous animals—including those of the canine species—to be euthanized. Although this guide covers certain pertinent sections of law which often create pitfalls for werewolves, it is by no means extensive or should be treated as legal advice. Therefore, if you or a loved one are facing charges while Lycan in New York, call an experienced and dedicated criminal defense lawyer to protect your constitutional rights.

CONNECT WITH GHOULISH BOOKS EVERYWHERE.

SATURN DEVOURING HIS SON

Nina Maar

JUNIOR LOVED HER parents. So much so that every night at exactly 6PM, she would sit on the table in the kitchen with the plastic tablecloth and wait in complete and utter silence for her mother and her father to come home from work and eat her alive. Every night they would tear her limb from limb, gobble up her organs and meat, and gnaw on her bones. Every night she would die, and in the morning she would wake up again, remade whole, to the sound of her alarm clock. As long as her mother and father tucked her bones into her bed at night, they could continue to devour Junior for dinner again and again and again.

Today on the kitchen table the sun was setting at a strange angle and it bathed Junior in a warm golden light. She sighed, thankful for the sun's warm hug in her final moments. Junior had spent many, many years adjusting herself to her parents' particular tastes. Her mother did not like it when Junior questioned why she had to be eaten—then she was 'spoiled', as her mother called it, and it made her taste sour. Her father did not like Junior when she was loud, when she cried, when she talked back to him, when she was as stubborn as he. He thought that she was 'disgusting' then, and would pick at her like a vulture rummaging through scraps, eating half-heartedly. Neither of them was particularly fond of Junior when she was anything other than pliant and quiet. So it was what Junior had become.

She heard the front door click open and the voices of her parents drift into the hallway as they took off their coats and shoes and keys. Sometimes her parents threatened Junior into silence by telling her that they would throw her bones out into the trash, or out in the patio, or far away in the woods, and she would die. Junior had bowed a heavy head then. Dying was different than being eaten, her parents had explained. If she died then she'd never come back, but if they ate her every night then Junior could live forever.

Her mother's quick footsteps traveled down the hall and into the kitchen. Junior looked in her general direction, but none of them ever really made any eye-contact anymore.

"Hi, my love," her mother said. Junior could feel the smile on her face.

Her mother was, to Junior at least, the most beautiful woman who had ever lived, and who would ever live after that. She worked in the realm of charm and trickery, and she worked it very well. Junior herself, often allowed her mother to do anything to her when she cupped her cheeks in soft, warm hands. Her father's footsteps made the floor tremble, and when he entered the kitchen the entire room seemed to shrink. Junior tucked her head slightly into her shoulders. Junior's father was fastidious and smart, so he worked high up in the government, typing away numbers and equations and codes all day. He would come home most nights angry at the world, and hungry enough to swallow it whole. When he screamed at Junior, she thought that the house was going to collapse.

"Are you going to sit down or are you just going to stare at her the whole time?" her father asked her mother.

Junior knew that her mother and father did not like each other very much. They *had* liked one another once upon a time, but she had not been born then and in truth, Junior could not comprehend the idea of a time in which her parents might have been in love. They only came together at dinner time.

Her mother rolled her eyes and took her seat at the table. There were only two chairs, because they allowed no guests over, and Junior's mother always sat to the left. Her father took his seat on the right. They each took their cutlery without a word, and Junior's mother allowed her father to make the first cut, sensing his anxiety. He cut into her leg at the knee, making quick work of severing the whole thing off. Junior knew that he liked her limbs the most, and parts like her diaphragm and liver. He liked meat that he could hold in his hands like a burger, meat that exploded with blood inside his mouth. Junior's mother sliced a chunk out from her belly. She preferred the soft stomach area, and crunchy chewy bits such as Junior's fingers, ears, ribs, and nose.

Junior thought that being eaten hurt, but it was a kind of pain that had turned into a fog within her own mind. She did not remember another kind of life, she was positive that there had never been one at all. It hurt that her parents ate her, and the metal blade stung her entire body, but she kept the pain mostly at bay, even if it burned. She hurt because she hoped that if she could do nothing else correctly in their eyes, at least she could allow them to eat her, and yet they had begun to bite down on her flesh begrudgingly in recent months, and sometimes Junior had to hold back her tears. As her parents consumed more and more of her, Junior began to fall into a deep sleep. By the time her father cracked her ribcage open she was already long-gone. Her parents always split the lungs, heart, and brain between one another. Around 10PM, when there was only a whittling pile of bones left on the table, Junior's mother gathered them all together while her father washed the dishes. She carried them up the stairs and down the hall into Junior's room, where she laid them gently down on Junior's bed. Then she shut the door behind her and retired to her own room for the night.

***

When Junior awoke the next morning, both of her parents had already left for work. Her body felt as it always did, stiff and aching. She sighed deeply, and thought for a second about skipping school and laying under the covers all day. Her mother would always dry her sheets and blankets in the dryer to ensure that they were soft and fluffy so it made getting out of bed very hard for Junior. Her father hated wasting money on things he deemed useless, so he rarely allowed the heat to be on, and Junior's room was the coldest one in the house. A birdsong was heard from the outside, and it reminded Junior that there was indeed still a world beyond her own home, so she quickly rose out of bed and into the bathroom to get ready for the day.

Junior waited for the school bus every day at the same stop two blocks down from her house. Her parents had sent her to a prestigious private institution in hopes of looking like they cared, and maybe in hopes of Junior growing up to become richer than God. She excelled in school because she had always been told by her parents that she was smart, so smart she became. Junior was not at the top of her class because she did not want to be, things like that attracted too much attention to herself, and it made her stomach churn. She heard the bus approaching and adjusted her backpack on her shoulders. When the bus stopped, she climbed into it swiftly, mumbling a small 'good morning' to the driver, and sitting down toward the front end of the bus. Since she was one of the first children who got picked up, she sat towards the front to allow room for the rest of her more rambunctious classmates to horse around at the back.

She slept lightly for a bit, semi-aware of the bus filling up until she felt a gentle tap on her shoulder. When she opened her eyes, her friend Halley was struggling to set her own backpack down in her lap.

"Hi Junie," Halley said.

"Hi," Junior replied.

Once Halley managed to settle down in her seat she turned to Junior properly, running a hand through her hair.

"Did you hear what happened?" Halley asked, her voice suddenly much quieter.

Junior shook her head. She was often uninterested in gossip and other people's lives, only keeping tabs on the interior lives of her handful of friends and the occasional happenings through the grapevine. Halley smiled, a thin tight line across her face that told Junior she was excited to share this information with her. Halley really did not care about the information she overheard, but she loved to share other people's business and misfortunes. Halley leaned in closer, her arm flush against Junior's sweater.

"They found Boo Francis. Dead in his own room, under his own bed. They say his parents didn't want him anymore."

One by one, as Halley's words settled into Junior's mind, the vertebrae of her spine moved closer together, and she became as stiff as a log. She didn't know Boo Francis, a boy a handful of years older than her, but she'd grown familiar with the missing person posters with his face on them. He'd been missing now for almost a month. For the poster his parents had chosen a picture of him holding a soccer trophy. She turned her head to Halley with a practiced look of mild shock on her face.

"No way," Junior said. Her voice steady.

"Yes way."

"How did they kill him?" Junior asked.

Halley said nothing. On her face was the smile of a sly fox. Junior asked again.

"How was it, Halley?"

"They beat him up. They beat him up so *bad* all of his organs ruptured inside him and he drowned in his own blood. Then they stuffed him under his own bed, and I don't think he'd ever been found if not 'cuz the smell got so bad the neighbors complained."

Junior furrowed her eyebrows. "The cops didn't search his room first?"

Halley shrugged, sat back down in her seat and began to mess with her nails. Junior knew that meant she had delivered all the information she knew—anything else was left up to the imagination. Junior turned to the window of the bus then, watching the houses and the lawns fly past. Boo Francis did not deserve to die, Junior *knew* this. But a knot at the base of her skull told her that maybe he did. Maybe Boo Francis was also spoiled and disgusting like her, and so his parents had to kill him.

Maybe they had been merciful enough to eat his soul instead.

***

As Junior sat on the kitchen table that evening, she tried to recall if her parents had any recent pictures of her in case she went missing, and she tried and failed to imagine the pain of all of her organs exploding.

***

The next morning, Junior awoke to a bleak and chilly room. She felt a presence at the far end of her bed. Cautious of her parents, she took her covers off slowly, and she sat up to find a boy a handful of years older than herself wearing their school's soccer uniform. He was curled at her feet like a dog. Junior could not really call the red and purple mush a face anymore, and the rest of his body was lumpy and twisted in all sorts of wrong directions. He had no eyes, but she knew that he was looking at her still. Small clouds of hot breath floated out from his crooked jaw. It was too far to the left, teeth no longer aligning, but his voice emerged from his body clear as day.

"Time's running out, you gotta start eating them back."

Junior did not say anything, feeling that she'd burst into tears if she did, and they sat in insufferable silence until Boo Francis sat up and began to paw his way around her bed. His head swerved around with a jarring motion, as if he was still trying to see where he was. Eventually he found the side rail of her bed and he managed to crawl down onto the floor face first. He twisted and turned his body around to fit back under Junior's bed and was gone. Junior remained in her bed for a while. She realized that she had no favorite foods, and that she herself was too big to slide under her bed like Boo Francis had. As she rode the bus to school that morning, Junior's breath came short.

***

When her mother cut open into her cheek that night, the familiar drowsiness stilled her uneasy heart. Her arms and legs were gone at this point, and her guts were rapidly disappearing. She tightened her eyes shut and forced them back open again, willing herself to stay awake past the point in which the pain usually made her vision go dark. Boo Francis' words kept playing back inside her head, haunting her. It seemed stupid to her now, that she'd never questioned if the time would ever come when her parents got tired of eating her—and then what? and then what? She knew their threats were as empty as their stomachs were full, but she'd never thought of her life being anything else. It was just not possible. Her diaphragm cramped as she thought about a life unlike this one. Her mother poked her to stay still. Junior realized she'd never eaten dinner before.

In her eternal silences as she waited on the kitchen table, Junior often hoped and prayed and even dreamt for the day in which her mother and her father would both cradle her gently and settle her down onto a chair by their side, and they could all eat together instead of this—

Maybe.

Junior willed her eyes to open again.

If she managed to stay awake for once it could prove . . . something. Maybe she would open her eyes and she'd be whole again instantly. Maybe her mother and father would be so impressed by her resilience they would stop eating her. Maybe she'd wake up in her bed, having ended a terrible dream. If nothing else, it could prove that her parents could not get away with murder like Boo Francis' parents had tried, and it would ease Junior's anxieties a little. Her father made a vanishing act of her intestines, and Junior held very still as her mother plunged a fork into her left eye and twisted it around a few times like spaghetti to set it loose. It was harder to stay awake with her eyes gone, so she decided to focus on the sound of her parents chewing. Crunching sounds told her that her fingers were gone. She braced herself for the feeling of her father cracking open her ribs, and when he did it a gasp died in her throat because she did not have one anymore. She felt a pain unlike anything before. A flash of hot red that raced up and down what was left of her spine. She could feel the blood pooling below her tongue. She thought of Boo Francis' heart bursting like a million fireworks.

***

Suddenly she found herself nowhere in particular, and everywhere inside her own home. Like she'd become a blanket of snow, gently wrapping around the walls of her abode. Maybe this was how ghosts felt. Only a thought drifting about the tangible world. Was she now the sum of her soul? She was somewhere above it all, attached only by a thread. She watched with eyes that were not her own as her mother and father piled her bones onto a different plate and argued for a second about who would do the dishes this time. Her mother stayed in the kitchen while her father took the plate upstairs.

Her father walked into her room and settled her bones into bed. He adjusted her pillow and threw the covers over them. He turned the light off and mumbled a small 'goodnight Junie' as he closed the door. She felt the strings of her non-existent heart tighten. She'd never heard her father say goodnight to her before. She was not sure if this meant he knew that she was not dead, or if he often spoke to her bones, but it did not comfort her in the way she'd liked.

When her father's heavy footsteps receded further away from her bedroom, she drifted down towards her bed, less like a cloud and more like a sopping wet paper towel. Her bones trembled with a degree of anticipation she'd never felt before. She could hear the electricity coursing through them. When Junior opened her eyes again, she was in her bed, gently tucked under the covers, and it was still dark outside. The moon, which Junior rarely managed to see, hung high in the sky, seemingly watching her move about for the first time. Her forehead was sticky with sweat.

She hesitated for a moment then, listening for her father's footsteps or her mother's laugh, but there was nothing. Junior took a deep breath, then rose up and out of her bed. She stood still again, legs unsure, body tender, soul raw. Boo spoke from under her bed.

"Time's running out, you gotta start eating them back."

"I could," she replied in a soft voice. "But they eat me for every dinner, and I come back every single time."

"Then what?" Boo asked.

"I could beat them," Junior said. "But yours beat you and you came back too."

"That they did." Boo laughed like a dead dog. "Shoulda shoved me further under my bed, woulda taken me longer to come back out."

Junior's own stomach rumbled and she set out towards the stairs. Boo Francis followed behind her silently on all fours. In the kitchen Junior opened the fridge to find it empty. *Eat them back,* she thought. *How how would I ever*

She walked down the hall to the laundry room. Boo did not follow. At the back of the bottom cupboards her mother kept a big dark plastic bottle that Junior had seen her pour into one of the holes of their car's engine. Inside was a bright green liquid. Junior took it and brought it back to the kitchen, where she climbed onto the plastic tablecloth. Boo Francis snuck back underneath. Junior twisted the cap open and the sweet smell of syrup wafted around her nose, sticking to her skin. She brought it up close to her mouth and took a swig. Then another and another.

***

When the sun rose, Junior's parents awoke to find her dead atop the kitchen table. Puffy white foam spilled from her mouth and her nostrils, and she was cold to the touch.

"Oh my goodness!" her mother said. "Do you think she's still edible like this?"

"Maybe," her father replied. "We could barbecue her if she's too tough to chew."

"A soup would work too, it would soften the meat."

And so her mother and her father set out to dismember Junior into smaller pieces and cook what they could. Her father grilled her arms and legs. Her mother threw her liver and her hands into a pot of vegetables. They boiled her eyes and fried her tongue, and they inhaled the sweet sickly smell of meat and loved it. Once all of her meat had been stripped from her bones and all of her bones had been cooked into broth, her mother and her father sat down at the kitchen table to eat.

"We should cook like this more often," her mother said.

"I guess so," her father said. "We could do it on the weekends."

They ate Junior with much gusto. Enjoying every bite, having seasoned her with the best spices and lots of butter. Her mother spread the paste she'd made from Junior's guts across a slice of bread. Her father slurped noisily as he drank down the last of the broth. By the time they finished eating Junior, the sun had already set once more. Her father let out a low whistle.

"I should fix up the washing machine, it's a pain to wash so many plates."

"And you have to wipe down the grill too, don't forget," her mother teased.

Junior's father rolled his eyes as he made to stand up from the table, but then a sharp pain hit his side and he promptly sat back down. He cleared his throat.

"What's wrong, honey?" Junior's mother asked.

He did not reply. His stomach rumbled and his breathing became short.

"Must be your acid reflux," she said. "I'll go get you something."

***

Junior's mother stood from the table and stumbled backwards, her legs weak. She walked backwards, and bumped against the sink. Junior's father began to cough, his throat was dry, and his nose seemed to be stuffed because he could feel no air traveling through his chest. Dinner poked him in the side of the abdomen again. Junior's mother slipped to the ground with a small smack. She tried to speak but no words came from her mouth, instead she groaned in pain like a wild beast. She felt air bubbling up across her guts and a heaviness settled at the bottom of her lungs. From somewhere deep within herself she felt a small kick. Junior's father bent over the kitchen table suddenly, gripping the plastic tablecloth with one hand and his stomach with the other. He tried to tear at the buttons of his shirt to no avail. His skin pressed tighter and tighter against his clothes. Within his body something grew and grew, shifting the position of his organs. Junior's mother arched backwards, her spine snapping taut. Her hands curled inward, each joint in her fingers cracking with a resonance. She threw her head back, hitting herself against the edge of the counter. Thick, dark, black and red blood erupted from her open mouth, back down onto her face and from within her something dragged its nails across her ribs. Junior's father pushed the table away, his stomach bulging over the belt of his pants, his face and his hands swollen red, purple, and pink. On the floor, Junior's mother thrashed her arms and legs every which way, banging her head onto the counter with no particular sense of rhythm. Junior's father felt another punch to the gut, and then another, and another. He clawed at his shirt frantically, begging, praying, pleading for the pain to stop. Junior's mother heard the sound of a tree branch breaking and a wave of red hot heat traveled up from her chest to her temple. Then another and another, one by one her ribs broke in half, allowing for more room. Something inside her writhed. It twisted and turned, and she along with it. Somewhere through her cloud of pain, Junior's mother heard her husband gag and choke. Junior's father began to shake in his seat, his arms and legs flailing. A long, sharp sting traced the inside of his stomach lining, causing it to slowly split open. Junior tore layer by layer of meat. Through her mother and her father she clawed her way out. Wading upwards through their hatred and gore, scratching away at their throats, lungs, and hearts.

***

The next morning Junior awoke on the floor of the kitchen remade anew.

She opened the fridge to find fruits and vegetables, milk, sweet tea, eggs, and ham. She cracked an egg along the counter and swallowed it raw. Then she fed one to Boo, careful to wipe the corner of his crooked jaw. She ate the rest herself. She took out the rest of the food in the fridge and laid it out atop the plastic tablecloth. Boo crawled up onto a chair as best he could. Junior ate all the ham and drank all the tea. She would clean up her mother and her father later.

How does Libro.fm work?

Libro.fm makes it possible for you to buy audiobooks through our bookstore. But how?

Profits from your monthly membership and à la carte audiobook purchases are shared with our bookstore.

Libro.fm requires no extra work and no money on the bookstore's end. Why? Because they want more money in local communities, where it can make the greatest impact.

When you sign up to support our bookstore with a Libro.fm membership, you provide us with sustained, reliable income over time, so we can stay serving the community—and keeping the lights on.

And you'll enjoy curated playlists and recommendations from expert booksellers like us, along with a simple and thoughtful listening platform.

https://libro.fm/indie-partners/resources?bookstore=ghoulishbookstore

ABOUT OUR GHOULS

Robert Nazar Arjoyan was born into the Armenian diaspora of Glendale, California. Aside from an arguably ill-advised foray into rock n roll bandery during his late teens, literature and movies were the vying forces of his life. Naz graduated from USC's School of Cinematic Arts and now works as an author and filmmaker.

Nicholas A. Battaglia is a lawyer appointed to the NYS Supreme Court, Appellate Division, Third Judicial Department, and began writing horror during the pandemic as an outlet and to relax. His publications evolved from appearing in the American Bar Association (ABA), New York State Bar Association (NYSBA), and in peer-reviewed journals, to now crawling through the pages of several horror anthologies, including with Hellbound Books, DarkLit Press, Sley House, Culture Cult, Haunted MTL, Timber Ghost Press, and *Hallowzine Issue 2* (nonfiction article). He haunts upstate New York with his wife, baby boy, and dog, and plans on finishing his first novella in 2023. Follow him on Twitter "Nick Writes Law and Horror" @nickthelawyerNY, or visit his website www.NABattaglia.com.

Barbara Castro-Rojas writes cosmic and sci-fi-horror. Her poetry book, *Anywhere but Here*, was independently published in 2018. In 2020, her feature film script, *Mujeres*, was a finalist in the Austin After Dark competition. Barbara graduated from the University of St Andrews with a degree in International Relations and has been trying to redeem herself ever since. She works in the video game industry.

Clay McLeod Chapman writes books, comic books, children's books, and for film/TV. You can find him at www.claymcleodchapman.com.

Lor Gislason (they/them) is an autistic non-binary homebody from Vancouver Island, Canada and the editor of *Bound in Flesh: An Anthology of Trans Body Horror*. Their articles have been featured on *Hear Us Scream, Horror Obsessive* and several upcoming anthologies. Their dream is to one day make an encyclopedia covering body horror films. Their novella, *Inside Out*, is available wherever goopy books are sold.

Chloé Harper Gold is a lifelong devotee of all things spooky, macabre, and grotesque. Her story "Starlight and Fairy Dust" was published in Crystal Lake Publishing's *Shallow Waters Volume IV,* and her drabbles "God Given Duty," "Snake Bite," and "Cradle to Grave" can be found in Reanimated Writers Press' *100-Word Zombie Bites*. Her short film "Final Pickup" premiered at Screamfest LA in 2021 and has since played in several other film festivals including Chicago Horror Film Festival and Anti-Hero Fest. Chloé has also written for *Nightmarish Conjurings, Dread Central, Horror Film Central, 71 Magazine, Honeysuckle Magazine, Adweek, High Times*, and *SuperRare*.

Rae Knowles (she/her) is a queer woman with multiple works forthcoming from Brigids Gate Press. Her debut novel, *The Stradivarius*, is coming May '23, her sapphic horror novella, *Merciless Waters*, is due out winter '23, and her collaboration with April Yates, *Lies That Bind*, in early '24. A number of her short stories have been published or are forthcoming from publications like *Dark Matter Ink, Nightmare, Seize the Press, Taco Bell Quarterly*, and Nosetouch Press. Recent updates on her work can be found at RaeKnowles.com and you can follow her on twitter @_Rae_Knowles

Angela Liu is a Chinese-American writer from NYC. She researched mixed reality at Keio University's Graduate School of Media Design in Japan and now works in IT consulting (while taming a kaiju-obsessed toddler). Her stories and poetry are published/forthcoming in *Strange Horizons, Maudlin House, The Dark, Nightmare Magazine, Fusion Fragment, Clarkesworld, Dark Matter Magazine*, among others. Read more of her work at: https://liu-angela.com. Or find her on Twitter and Instagram @liu_angela

Nina Maar is an amateur writer and illustrator with a penchant for the color periwinkle, horror media, and candles with pictures of saints on them. They have recently obtained a bachelor's degree and are currently focusing on their writing, aiming for grad-school, or descending into complete and utter insanity.

Betty Rocksteady spends as much time as possible wandering around daydreaming. Her illustrated cosmic sex horror novella *The Writhing Skies* won the 2018 This is Horror Award for best novella, and was nominated for the Splatterpunk Award. Surreal and explicit, her short fiction is collected in *In Dreams We Rot*. Her illustration style is inspired by old cartoons and newspaper comics. Her first graphic novel, *Soft Places*, was published in 2002. Find out more at www.bettyrocksteady.com.

DO YOU WANT TO WRITE FOR GHOULISH TALES?

We will reopen for Ghoulish Tales Issue #2 on July 15th and close on August 15th. Writers are encouraged to submit their best stories to ghoulishsubmissions@gmail.com with [TITLE] – [LAST NAME] – [STORY/ESSAY] in the subject line. Please do not copy/paste the story in the body of the email. We prefer Word doc attachments if possible. All inquiries can also be directed to the same address. Stories received before July 15th or after August 15th will be deleted unread. For an idea of what we are looking to publish, please refer to the stories in the issue you are currently holding in your hands.

Word count: 5,000 max (short stories) 3,000 max (non-fiction); Payment: 10c per word; Simultaneous Submissions: Yes; Multiple Submissions: No; Reprints: No.

GHOULISH TALES

ISSUE 2 | AUTUMN 2023

If You Don't Buy This Magazine, We'll Kill This Ghoul